Christopher, a quiet, reserve
restaurants and night clubs in
and nervous breakdown in the ..., ...
spiritual possession-free life on the Mediterranean island.

Lucas flees an abusive ex in Madrid to live his dream of
dancing in Ibiza's large prestigious night clubs.

They meet at a night club and both feel an instant attraction
which soon develops into an emotional connection neither
of them feels ready for.

Sharing their painful pasts with each other brings them
closer together, though neither of them planned on being in
a proper relationship. But when a family crisis pulls Lucas
back to Madrid and a painful encounter with his abusive ex,
Christopher deals with painful experiences of his own.

THE JOURNALIST
AND THE DANCER

Liam Livings

A NineStar Press Publication

Published by NineStar Press
P.O. Box 91792,
Albuquerque, New Mexico, 87199 USA.
www.ninestarpress.com

The Journalist and the Dancer

Printed in the USA
First Edition
October, 2018

Print ISBN: 978-1-949909-20-3

Also available in eBook, ISBN: 978-1-949340-82-2

Chapter One

"WHAT ARE YOU drinking?" the barman asked. He wore a low v-neck sleeveless T-shirt and looked far too skimpily dressed for what was purporting to be another straight bar.

"Gin and tonic. Large." Christopher winked—it was always worth a try wherever he was, and Ibiza's bars were very mixed anyway. Straights and gays shared most drinking establishments happily. A relationship of equals, was that too much to want?

He checked the invite, scanning down for anything unusual. Among the rubbish about it being the new place to be seen on the island and where all the *it* people hung out, whoever they were—Christopher had lived on Ibiza for a year or so and had yet to meet these so-called *it* people— were pictures of men and women laughing and drinking together, so probably aiming for the straight crowd.

"Excuse me. We've run out of soda water. Can I get you something else?" The barman shook the hose contraption and shrugged.

"Surprise me." *Because nothing else here is surprising.* The red walls were covered in likenesses of the island's shape, with large white skulls painted on either end, and the dark corners of the club were filled with silver chairs and tables. The latest Eurotrash track boomed from the stage on the far side of the room. Christopher stifled a yawn. Somehow, this wasn't quite what he'd imagined looking for a less materialistic life would be like.

But he still had to eat.

The barman slid a tall, multicoloured cocktail adorned with a blue umbrella and red cherry along the bar. "Surprise!"

Christopher took a sip and was pleasantly shocked that he enjoyed the bitter sweetness. "When is the actual opening happening?"

"Eight, eight thirty." The barman talked enthusiastically about the cannons, which were going to spurt white foam over the revellers on the dance floor.

"Foam cannons? Really?" *I think the year 2000 called and it wants its nightclub back.* Christopher rolled his eyes behind the tall cocktail glass.

"It's not a club here without one—apparently." The barman shrugged and his biceps rippled in the light. "Mind you, have you seen the cages hanging above the dance floor?"

"Where?"

The barman pointed through an archway to the source of the pulsing noise that passed as music here.

Bit tacky. How can I say it's a bit tacky without actually saying it's a bit tacky? How about fanciful? Or maybe enthusiastic? Christopher pondered the right words for a few moments.

The barman left to serve another customer, tiny white shorts about two sizes too small encased his tight arse cheeks—definitely a good seven or an eight—wiggling as he walked.

Christopher contemplated what a waste that arse was on a straight man, then pulled a white wafer-thin laptop from his bag and began writing his *Ibiza Discovered* review for yet another nightclub opening. *If I ask the barman a few more questions, that, and a few words about the ambiance—always deathly dull at these things—I'll be done and home to chill out with the TV and Sally within the hour. Maybe that's why I'm still single. Or maybe it's because I don't think I'll ever find a man who's equal to me...*

"The VIP area is ready when you are." A slight man in a black suit with sweat on his brow appeared at Christopher's shoulder.

With a sinking feeling that his *leaving within the hour* plan was looking less likely now, he followed the man to an area with a red velvet rope and clipboard-checking woman who flicked her long brown hair more often than she checked the guest list.

Christopher gave his name, waited as the woman checked it and was then shown to a table with other people talking and toasting with champagne.

People. And they're talking. They're going to want to talk to me and want to know who I...Damn!

"Who are you reviewing for?" a man at the table asked.

"*Ibiza Discovered.*" Different people asking the same questions, probably going to suggest the same bloody drinking game as the evening progressed. Being this standoffish was definitely not improving his chances of finding a date any time soon, he realised.

After introductions around the table—a few local papers, a website mag, and a clubbing scene mag—Christopher gritted his teeth as the first man suggested they play a drinking game, based on how many times the manager said certain words in his welcome address.

He checked his watch. With no sign of the manager announcing the formal opening, and already half an hour late, his quiet evening plans were gradually disappearing, drink by drink.

One of the journalists was talking about the last club opening he'd been to, something about a fire alarm and how they'd all ended up in the... Christopher's attention drifted from the man's story to a gentlemen who skipped and floated across the dance floor. Nothing too unusual so far, but the fact that he was wearing only a pair of tight gold trunks with glitter over his athletic hairless chest made Christopher sit up, his shorts tighten, and his stomach flutter.

The man shouted, "*Me cago en tu puta madre!*" and turned to face Christopher, staring for what seemed like a minute, smiling and not breaking eye contact.

Christopher couldn't take his eyes off this exotic passionate creature, staring so intensely and deeply it felt as if he were staring into his soul. He knew that no man dressing like that would take himself too seriously. He felt sure that a man like that would humour his partner, was comfortable with himself fully without censoring, wouldn't mock every decision of other people like... Christopher stopped that particular avenue of memories.

Then, as suddenly as he'd arrived, the man shook his head, clapped twice, and ran through a door to the side of the stage.

That arse in those trunks was at least a nine, possibly a ten. Who is he? What's the English equivalent to that sweary Spanish phrase? Where is he going? And why aren't I talking to him instead of this group of idiots?

LUCAS SLAMMED THE dressing room door and, in an attempt to regain his composure, tried to slow down his breathing. That last-minute dash across the dance floor had revealed there was more press than he'd expected for a crappy little club like this. At least he assumed they were the press—the table of men in grey suits in the VIP area, shouting and drinking champagne. They looked like journalists. Not that he knew much about what journalists looked like, but anyway.

All except one, who, with his T-shirt and shorts and neatly trimmed blond beard, looked like a holidaymaker. A holidaymaker with piercing blue eyes and a smile that had made Lucas want to lick his lips and set his heart racing. Even now, he remembered the stare.

That stare they'd shared for a perfect moment.

Blond Guy seemed lonely despite his casual clothing. Lucas wondered if the man didn't want to be there—maybe he was missing his partner or something. Lucas hadn't been able to think of much else except Blond Guy since noticing him. He felt...something, a pull, an attraction, a something towards this man, and it wasn't just lust. Those blue eyes, that blond hair, the cute trimmed beard, the stocky build all sent jolts to Lucas's groin. He looked so different from all the Spanish men on the island. Maybe he would also be different from the Spaniards too... And that smile, the look they'd shared—Lucas had felt a connection, a draw to the man. Without even talking to him, Lucas admired how he refused to dress grey-corporate like the other journalists. Maybe not love at first sight, but certainly lust and an attraction pulling them together.

Blond Guy was cute and an individual, clearly different from so many other men he found attractive, and Lucas knew how rare that was.

Concentrate.

A knock on the door woke Lucas from his thoughts about Blond Guy.

The manager burst through the door with no pause for Lucas's reply. "I told you, no glitter, no gold hot pants, none of this—" The manager seemed to search for the right word. He clicked his fingers a few times, ruffled the feathers in one of Lucas's costumes. "—this camp. It is not bloody Mardi Gras. This is not one of *your* sort of clubs. This is respectable, classic, classy. Or at least that's what I'm going to say in my opening speech." He gestured grandly with both hands in the air. "I told you this already."

Lucas nodded, remembering the earlier briefing, but he'd hoped he could get away with it—otherwise why would he have been given the job?

"Butch up, will you?" He tapped Lucas's shoulders. "I know this isn't your first choice, but you weren't mine either, if that makes you feel any better. Money's money. So sort yourself out and get ready to sweep the women off their feet." He bustled out.

Lucas washed the glitter from his chest and changed into the Superman costume he'd been given, pinning it at the back to prevent the *S* on the chest sagging into a sad sort of *I*.

He couldn't deny that money was indeed money, but it hadn't stopped him hoping, wishing, praying, that tonight would turn from a tryout to something more permanent, or that someone in the audience would spot him and pluck him from obscurity to the mainstream so he could fulfil his life-long dream of dancing for a living. And now his mind wandered back to him, Blond Guy. Those thighs in those shorts. Those biceps from that T-shirt. Different. Quirky. Twinkly smile.

CHRISTOPHER HAD EXTRICATED himself from the drinking game and other journalists and was now chatting to a barmaid who'd made him another of the tall colourful cocktails.

"What about the dancers?" Christopher asked, steadying himself against the bar and trying to focus on his laptop screen, and failing. He used all his concentration and worked out the time was 9:30, an hour after the manager was meant to be opening with his long-awaited speech.

"What *about* the dancers?" the barmaid asked. "They dance. In cages. Above the dance floor." She beckoned him closer. "Come, see. I will show you."

The Superman theme tune filled the club.

Christopher yawned so hard he almost fell off his barstool. He packed up his things and walked towards the door. *How cheesy. How eighties. How tacky. I'm off to bed.* Who would have thought that leaving the rat race for this life in sun-kissed Ibiza would mean a different race but the same rats? He'd left his banking job in London and wanted to take things down a notch, to simplify but not so simple he could feel his brain ossifying from boredom.

The crowd cheered and Christopher shook his head. There was no accounting for taste, that was for sure. He turned to take one quick picture of the club to help with writing the review later when a man in a Superman costume flew across the stage, right to left, with his cloak fluttering behind him in the breeze generated from a large fan off stage. The effect was somewhat spoilt by Superman then flying backwards left to right, across the stage as his cloak covered his face.

The sight of Superman so obviously suspended by wires, swinging from left to right on the stage, while he remained deadpan, was too much for Christopher to maintain a straight face. So Christopher laughed.

During the last swing back to the right side of the stage, Superman turned, made eye contact with Christopher, and smiled back.

Christopher recognised the dancer from earlier and mourned the covering of all the tantalising glitter-covered flesh that had been on display by the ridiculous sagging outfit. Christopher waved at the dancer, not believing where that had come from, and quickly sat on his hand in embarrassment.

The dancer waved at him and Christopher found himself smiling, staring into deep dark eyes. Poor man, he was obviously much better than this Superman twaddle. *I wonder why he's not wearing the gold glittery skimpy outfit.* Wishing he'd taken a photo of the dancer's previous outfit, Christopher continued staring at the dancer who pulled the cape from his face and, with the slightest nod of the head, signalled how he really felt about this whole Superman charade.

A screen covered the stage as the silhouette of Superman continued to swing from side to side. The manager walked in front of the red curtain, coughed into a microphone, and asked if it was working.

"Thank you, ladies and gentlemen. Welcome to the opening night of Ikon—the hottest classiest club destination in Ibiza. Sorry that Superman had to leave, but he's got to get back to Metropolis, speeding through the air like a... bullet?"

Christopher had seen and heard it all before. So, satisfied he had enough to write a review, he left for home, pausing momentarily to notice Superman waving at him while swinging from side to side once again.

Holding the gaze for another few moments, he enjoyed the smile—and was that a wink too—that Superman was shooting back at him.

IN THE EARLY hours of that morning—in another bar because half the evening in Ikon had been more than enough, without spending the whole of it there—Lucas and a few of the other dancers were talking and drinking.

"Why Superman? I don't understand." Lucas frowned.

"What would you have done?" Giovanni stared.

"A peacock. An elephant. A lion. With a big mane...and a long tall tail like a peacock. I don't know. I wanted something a bit more—fun. Sometimes, I feel like an animal and I can move like a cat. You want to see?" Without waiting for a response, Lucas threw himself on the floor and walked slowly on all fours, pretending to lick his hand before wiping it against his imaginary ears on top of his head.

"You could be in that musical. What's it called, with all the cats, singing and dancing? It's been on all over the world."

"*Cats*?" Lucas took his seat again.

"That's the one." Giovanni, who'd somehow designated himself in charge, checked everyone's drinks. "Who's staying for another?"

"Better not. Who knows when I'll get another job?" Lucas stared at his drink, feeling pretty dejected and downtrodden by the whole experience.

"Didn't the manager ask you back?"

"Nope. Said I had done him okay when he was stuck for anyone else to do it, but that next time he wanted someone who could actually fill the costume. Big, broad and full of muscles is what he really wanted." Lucas shook his head. "Bloody Superman. Tacky or what?"

"I'll get this. He asked me back. Want me to put in a good word for you?" He raised his eyebrows slightly.

"Will it change my body shape?" He'd trusted the manager when he'd said more would come from tonight's tryout dance. He'd believed tonight would be the start of something big; something more than scrabbling about for work and borrowing money off friends and promising he'd buy the next meal or round of drinks.

Giovanni returned with some churros—long fried Spanish doughnuts—and a bowl of melted chocolate. "These may change your body shape yet."

Lucas shuffled his chair closer and dipped the doughy goodness into the chocolate sauce. "It's silly, but can I ask you something?"

"Fire away."

"Did you notice the blond bearded guy with the journalists—he was the only one in T-shirt and shorts, and well, I think he was staring at me. I think he may have been laughing at me when I flew across the stage. Did he? I may be imagining it. The lights were bright. And I was nervous. But I'm sure I noticed him checking me out. And I think he waved too." *And I waved back, hopefully, entranced by his smile.*

"In that place? He waved, at you? Why would he be? Just another club opening. Just another stupid over-the-top launch show? He could go anywhere to see Superman flying across the stage. In fact, if he wanted to see a giant sea horse's head bursting into flames as someone flew into its mouth, he'd only need to go a few doors down to find it."

"Suppose not." Lucas rested his head in his hands and stuck his finger in the chocolate sauce, then absentmindedly licked it off.

"Oi! Dirty. No double dipping. Don't know where you've been." Giovanni smiled and handed Lucas a churro. "We dip this into the choc, okay?"

Lucas wasn't sure where he'd been, what he'd been doing, or why he'd been thinking about a man possibly maybe staring at him and waving at him and laughing at his disastrous performance in a straight night club. All wishful thinking. Wishful that the blond hair meant this man was the exact opposite of the dark-haired Spaniards he'd tried to date but failed. Wishful that the blond hair meant this man was Nordic or Australian or maybe British. Maria, his sister, had told him that Spanish men got bored quickly and that's where Lucas had been going wrong for all those years. He took one last, deep dip of the chocolate, waved his goodbyes, and left the others to it.

On his way home to Talamanca, a quiet bay only a short walk from the lights and bustle of Ibiza town, he replayed his swing across the stage and knew he had definitely seen Blond Guy checking him out. And waving briefly. And he in return had felt a something back. An attraction. The neatly trimmed beard and the biceps bulging from the T-shirt.

Guapo.

His younger sister, Maria, would understand his attraction to this *handsome man*. She knew all about love and lust at first sight, and fate, and people being made for each other. She and her husband proved it.

At times like this, he *almost* believed it could happen to him, that he could be lucky enough to find his perfect match. What else could explain his raised pulse, his dry throat at seeing Blond Guy, and his inability to forget about him after only a brief stare? All he'd been able to find with the other men was quick hookups and one or two dates that maybe ended in bed, or maybe a trailing off of texts and calls. Time and time again, Lucas wondered if perhaps what the homophobes said about men like him was right. He was sure he'd never have a family like his sisters and brothers with their husbands and wives. He was destined to be searching for the meaning of a possible shared look or a glance across a busy night club.

He was emotional and often rushed into things, but he knew what he'd seen and felt in the shared look between him and the blond man. There had been attraction and lust but also an emotional pull. The look, the wave, the stare. Sex was easy to find, love and sex was what Lucas really wanted. Why else would Blond Guy have stood out as the only man not wearing a grey suit? Anyone who came to a night club opening dressed like that would be laidback and the exact opposite of the reason he'd fled Madrid—his ex, Pedro.

At 6:00 a.m., as the sun was starting to rise, Lucas pulled the blinds in his small studio apartment, put his earplugs in and eye mask on, and snuggled up to his pillow. He wished it was someone lying next to him and hoping his situation wouldn't become so desperate that he'd have to return to only sex, when what he really longed for was love and sex.

He knew love could come from sex, but he also acknowledged he was probably looking for it in the wrong places. At the moment. He berated himself for not giving his number to Blond Guy. "Worth a try," Maria would surely have told him. This would have been an instance when not thinking before acting would have been useful. Only, his hesitation, too, showed him how much hope he'd already instilled in the brief encounter. If he didn't care either way, he'd have thrown his number out in the vague hope Blond Guy would call. Instead, he'd kept it to himself because at the moment the unrequited lust made Blond Guy perfect and unspoilt by reality. But he knew his mind wasn't replaying their first encounter again and again without good reason.

Chapter Two

CHRISTOPHER WAS SITTING on his balcony, his laptop and a coffee on the table in front of him, as Ibiza Town, the island's largest settlement, woke up. "I have a few questions I need to put to you," he asked Ikon's manager, "to make sure the article is correct." Although he was finding this whole process slightly tedious, it was at least—he reflected—sunny and going to continue to be for the foreseeable future.

"Fire away. Did you get that it was classy and classic with its own distinctive style?"

Christopher rolled his eyes. "We'll come to that. Now, what is the max capacity of the club? And I want to know about the sort of music you're planning to play there—surely the launch night wasn't indicative..."

The manager responded to the questions, each time, adding his own little twist and trying to remind Christopher of how classic and classy the club was. Christopher merely nodded and, in the end, typed—*irritating manager, avoid for future*—as a note to himself.

Christopher looked out across the port filled with private white boats the size of small houses, gently bobbing up and down in the water. "One last questions before I go; why the superheroes theme and how did that fit with the skulls?" The large white skulls that had been at either edge of the stage and had formed some of the seats and tables in the club. What on earth, Christopher wanted to know, had they been thinking of when they came up with that idea? The skulls had kept him awake when he returned home after the launch party. The skulls and the Superman. And the tiny glittery gold hot pants the dancer had worn before.

The vision of the dancer in those pants was what had eventually coaxed Christopher off to sleep in the early hours, as he remembered the smile and imagined what would lie beneath the pants.

The manager talked around the skulls issue trying to explain their significance being something linked to their day of the dead *Día de Muertos*, when they celebrated their dead relatives and had picnics on their graves, but it all seemed rather tenuous to Christopher. And on he talked.

Christopher stopped listening and instead remembered the dancer, the gold shorts and the Superman outfit. The gaze they'd shared, the wave to one another, had definitely been real. And the glitter on the hairless chest. How many times had he closed his eyes to remember it, to replay the smile in his mind? Why hadn't he left his business card for the dancer when he'd left the bar? Why hadn't he gone back stage and asked for the dancer there and then?

As usual, Christopher found himself regretting things he'd not done rather than anything he had done. Cautiousness was an overrated quality in some situations. Balling up his fists, he decided to try to be less cautious and follow his heart. But he didn't want to follow his heart to anyone. This was the first man he'd taken an interest in since arriving in Ibiza. Which made it even more idiotic that he'd up and left the club without getting the dancer's number.

Finally, the manager ended with, "I hope that's enough for you. If you don't mind, I have a night club to manage. Bye—"

Taking a deep breath, Christopher decided it was indeed now or never. "One more thing, before you go. Do you know the Superman guy? I mean, do you have his details so I can contact him? I—" He glanced around his balcony, desperate for a plausible reason to call the dancer. "—have a dancing job he would be perfect for." Christopher shook his head. Why hadn't he thought of this before he called? Why leave it until the last minute? Why was he so nervous? It had been a long time since he'd even wanted to look twice at any man and he knew it was more than lust—his fluttering heart at the shared look told him that.

"I can't give you his number. Besides, I only used him for that night. He won't be back. He wasn't really what I'm looking for."

"Oh." Christopher sighed loudly, covering the phone with his hand. Another opportunity missed. Another moment passed.

"Leave me your number and I'll pass it on. I'm sure I've got his number somewhere." There was a shuffling of paper as the manager sifted through the contents of his desk and drawers.

After Christopher gave his number, the manager signalled the call was over with a curt, "Done. Can I get on now? Some of us have work to do." The manager ended the call.

Christopher ran back into the flat where Sally was licking the foam off the top of her coffee while soaking her feet in a bowl of water.

"Do you think it's too soon?" Christopher flopped on the sofa next to her.

"What's too soon?" She sipped the coffee, flicking her dark bobbed hair over her ears.

"Getting this dancer's number? I feel ready to get back in the game now."

"Then you should give it a go. A year since the ex isn't too soon. What you got to lose?" She clicked her fingers. "Live a little. No, scrub that. Live a lot!"

"There was," Christopher said, leaning back on the sofa, "a definite spark in that wave and look. We stared at each other for what felt like hours. I know it was probably less than a minute, but it felt like it wasn't. You know?"

Sally bobbed her head from side to side and motioned for him to continue his story.

"I felt a something as soon as I saw him. I fancied him but more. And anyone dressing like that can't take himself too seriously. Who wouldn't mock others. Someone who's going to humour me, who won't mock everything I do. Sounds stupid now I've said it out loud." Christopher laughed.

"Not at all. I hate seeing couples taking the piss out of each other. Love, are you lonely?" That's what he loved about his flatmate, Sally. She always got straight to the point. She narrowed her eyes and sipped her coffee. "Continue."

Christopher shook his head. "I miss some parts of being a couple. The security. The knowing someone's always there. Someone who treats me as an equal. That would be a first." The hugs, the kisses, the companionship, the love, the sex...

Sally shook her head. "And do you think you might have that with Superman?"

"Maybe. I've not seen anyone else I'm interested in since... Could do." He shook his head. " I've not even spoken to him. It was...his look... Unconventional..Unlike my ex who never even wore costumes for fancy dress parties, never mind soaring across a stage as Superman. From what I saw, this man doesn't look like the sort who would mock me. Not dressing like that, he couldn't."

"It's not like an animal, love—you can't go searching for it with a pith helmet, a gun and a net over your shoulder it will—"

"Come to me, when I need it?" Christopher shrugged, hoping his gut instinct was right about the dancer. Being single after a seven year relationship had been great because until the night at the club no one had caught his eye, stood out to him. He'd not even looked twice at another man. Maybe it was because it felt as if the dancer would be exactly the opposite of his big burly buttoned up ex, and now Christopher had been single for long enough, he felt, with a degree of confidence, this dancer man might be worth the risk of another relationship. And the spark he'd felt and couldn't get out of his mind.

No way was the dancer going to be a dull corporate type. He was sure to be artistic, free, creative, interesting.

And really sexy.

Of course that helped too.

Sally stared at Christopher. "Love comes along when you least expect it, in my experience. I mean, look at me and Will?"

He had, indeed, spent the last few months looking at and listening to Sally and Will, much to his annoyance on a number of occasions. Running through the lounge with them sucking face all day. Walking past her bedroom with moans and bangs from the other side of the door. All at a point when Sally had declared she was off men and no matter what happened, she'd resist the charms of anyone. Until, that was, Will had been sent round by the landlord to fix their dodgy toilet cistern and had arrived with a bag of tools, a wide smile and a pair of biceps visible from a hundred yards.

"If he calls, he calls. I can do no more. The universe will make it so. Otherwise." Christopher shrugged, gently allowing himself a little hope that he had given the universe a helping hand by passing his number onto the club's manager. Maybe a little chant by his Buddhist shrine before bed, he'd allow himself just that too.

Never mind allow myself. I've no one mocking me this time, no waggling finger and disapproving looks from the ex to discourage me, I'll bloody well chant and sing and ring the bells to my heart's content if I want.

"I'm going to my room." He left the room for his bedroom and there sat quietly staring at his brass Buddha statue, lit a candle, sat cross-legged on the floor and practised his meditation until he felt satisfied he'd done all he could until the universe or the dancer would respond in their own time.

He just hoped that was sooner rather than later, because the hoping and the minor obsessing were proving exhausting.

ON THE OTHER side of Ibiza, Lucas sighed, staring into the greedy eyes of the man opposite him.

"The dancing must make you very flexible," the dark-haired Spanish man said, resting his hand on Lucas's.

"In some ways."

"Are we going to?"

"Do you want to?" Lucas wanted to, because, really, when was sex not a good idea for a man? But disappointingly, he was pretty sure it wouldn't lead anywhere. He knew that after the long dinner of small talk, the man opposite him had one thing and only that one thing on his mind. "I'd love to see you again." Lucas bit his lip and looked away. "My place is a fifteen-minute walk away."

"Mine's round the corner." The man held out his hand. "We can just talk. Nothing needs to happen."

So much for just talking. They'd barely made it through the front door of the man's apartment before his date had pounced and Lucas found himself arse up and filled with cock without so much as a pretence at being offered coffee first.

AFTERWARDS, AS THEY lay smoking cigarettes in bed, the man at one side and Lucas at the other, having been pushed away with a quick, "I don't cuddle," Lucas felt empty, relieved from sexual frustration, but still empty of love. Eventually, he'd enjoyed the sex, but the first few minutes had been pure pain, and despite calling out for the man to slow down, he'd continued thrusting deeper and harder into Lucas.

"We could get a coffee. What you doing Saturday lunchtime?" They'd worked together in bed, that had certainly been all right, eventually, and the conversation had been ticking along nicely.

"Why?" He folded his dark hairy arms across his chest.

"You said you'd want to see me again. You said it would be nice to carry on where we left off."

The man laughed, reached for his phone from the bedside table and began swiping left at icons of men's faces and bodies.

"Sunday?" Lucas asked.

"Busy."

"Which, Saturday or Sunday?"

"Err...both. Look, not being funny mate, but I'm not gonna waste my weekend on you, am I?"

Lovely. "Why?" Lucas pulled the sheets around his chest to cover himself.

"That's when I'm busiest. That's like first date time. Not for second dates."

"Right." Lucas was disappointed. How the man who'd been so charming earlier, and had promised him they'd meet up again, was now behaving like this. "We clicked."

"Yeah, we did. As in past tense. Done, over with. Look, are you gonna hang about for much longer, because I've got plans?"

"Sounds good, what are they?" Lucas looked up optimistically.

"Nothing you need to know about. Unless you fancy a threesome and some crystal?" He pursed his lips and looked Lucas up and down.

"I'd rather have a coffee with you on Saturday." Maybe not, now he'd mentioned drugs too. Where were the gay guys who wanted love and sex and not just sex, sex, and drugs?

"Not. Gonna. Happen." He pointed to the door. "Shower's through there."

Lucas stared at the man's lips that had a short time before been kissing his chest, cock, and balls. His eyes, that had looked so greedily at Lucas lying on his back as the same man had rolled a condom over his cock, lifted Lucas's legs over his shoulders and thrust into him for the second time that afternoon.

"Not being funny, but why would I bother with a second date, when I've already had you. I don't want a repeat of this. Boring! Like I said, unless you fancy a threesome I'm moving on. Bye. Have a nice life." He held Lucas's hands, moving closer on the bed. "No offence, but it's nothing against you—it's me. I just don't *do* second dates. I don't see the point. I usually get what I want on the first. I've only been in this place a month and I'm bored already. I'm on my third job this summer. I like to mix things up. Change them around." He kissed Lucas's lips, pausing to stick his tongue in and bite gently.

Maybe it was worth a try. Maybe he wasn't as bad as he seemed. Lucas leant forward, pushing himself against the man's chest, running his hands through the hairs, moving down to his navel, and cock which was by now stiffening.

The man pushed Lucas's hand away. "Not being funny, but I've got a date in an hour and I'm saving myself. Threesome and crystal? If not, you have a wank if you want. Use my Fleshlight. It's as good as an arse. But you're not a top, are you?"

That, Lucas now remembered, had been his opening question as they'd picked up their menus earlier that night. "Are you a top or a bottom?" he'd asked, without even a hello, my name is, or a how's your day been?

That should have been enough warning but, stupidly, Lucas had remained optimistic there would be more to him than simply being a top. And there was more to Lucas than being a bottom. Lucas opened his mouth to reply that he didn't think it was good to define yourself by one sexual act, how in his experience it varied between partners, situation, the emotions before and during the sex, so he didn't like to close himself off to other sorts of sex by sticking a label on himself like that, but then he realised he might as well tell that to the Fleshlight the man was now handing to him. Disappointed he'd mentioned the drugs again, realising this man really was how he appeared, no hidden depths, no hopes of romance as well as sex, and Lucas waved the Fleshlight away. He jumped out of bed, pulled on his clothes and grabbed his things, and waved the man goodbye.

As he stepped into the warm night Lucas realised he wasn't wearing any underwear. He enjoyed the feeling of freedom it gave him. *I'm so stupid. I'm so gullible. I'm so forgetful.* But he wasn't berating himself about the lack of underpants. He was walking quickly along the main road and shaking his head at jumping straight to the sex and skipping all the stuff he really missed about being in a relationship, therefore missing the opportunity for love.

He thought they'd clicked, but then realised they had, but only in bed, only just, and only twice. And then the drugs talk had turned him off. Again. So often the same in situations like this.

Looking for love in the wrong places, with the wrong men. Was he looking too hard?

Lucas video called his sister and told her what had just happened. He easily tumbled back into Spanish as soon as she answered. "*Hola!*"

"I saw you know who," Maria said with a tone of menace. "*That man* was asking after you."

"What did you say?" A sickness filled his body. A sickness mixed with an aching for the rare good times. Times he missed, unlike the rest of it.

"That you were dancing all over Ibiza and having a wonderful time. Did I do right?"

"Yes." He paused. "Even if it's not true."

"What happened to that club you worked at? Ikon gave you a regular dancing spot there, didn't they?"

Lucas nodded. They hadn't, but he didn't want to worry Maria. He knew it wouldn't have been the right sort of club for him. He didn't like how he couldn't choose his outfits and instead had to wear what was piled in his dressing room for him, pinning it tighter because he felt swamped in the costume's folds.

He bit his lip because he hated lying to her. "It's good. I'm so happy to be working there."

"Well then. Why do you look like that?" Maria frowned.

"I've got the guy's number. That journalist. Blond one. He's probably with his boyfriend at the moment, I expect."

"You don't know that about Blond Guy. It's all conjecture. He could be exactly who you need to get your name out to the rest of the island. One call from him and you'll be in demand everywhere. I think I know the answer to this, but I'm going to ask anyway. Have you called him yet?"

Lucas shook his head. "The manager—who by the way I hate because he's a bossy little jumped up man, thinks he knows what's best for me to wear—gave me his number; told me the Blond Guy had some dancing jobs he wanted to discuss with me. I've been thinking about it for a few days." Lucas had worried there would be some kind of catch to receiving Blond Guy's number. Then he'd moved onto excitement at talking to him, but still thought he'd call mañana—tomorrow. And then tomorrow had become today and Lucas wanted to put it off for another mañana. And then, he had become worried that Blond Guy wouldn't live up to his memories or expectations and he'd left it another mañana, and that had taken him up to today.

Unlike the random hookups, because he hadn't met Blond Guy through a dating app or in a gay club, Lucas felt it could mean something. Maybe, ironically, a straight club was the right place to look for love?

The anticipation of his hunch being right was stopping him from making the actual call. Because until he did so, the anticipation was perfect. Unlike how he was sure the reality would be.

Possibly.

But the reality of Blond Guy couldn't be any worse than the reality of the other guys he'd been spending time with, could it? Stupid as it sounded but Lucas felt more for Blond Guy from just that look than many men he'd slept with.

"No good thinking about it," Maria said. "A number's not going to ring itself. You need to ring it."

"I'll do it tomorrow." Lucas bit his lip.

"You always say that and then it becomes tomorrow and another tomorrow and before you know it, you've not done it and two weeks of tomorrows have passed."

Maria was right, but Lucas didn't want to admit that to her. "I left Madrid for here. If that was always tomorrow, I'd still be there."

"We both know why you left." Maria stared at her brother.

Lucas sighed. The breakup with his ex had been so painful that he'd needed to remove himself from not just Madrid, but also the whole country to prevent himself—like an injured dog returning to its abusive owner through habit—returning to the ex.

"You did the right thing," Maria said.

"Doesn't make it any easier." Lucas sighed. "I miss him. Is that the stupidest thing you've ever heard?" After the way he'd treated Lucas, it certainly seemed a ridiculous thing to say now he let the words fall from his mouth. Lucas had got used to the control, the violence, the endless complications and worries of upsetting Pedro. But he now knew that didn't make it right. He knew he wanted not only love, but a love that would allow him to flourish, to bloom, to dance through his life without disapproving looks. "You get used to being with someone, even if they hurt you," Lucas said. "There's comfort in familiarity."

"Even if that means being hurt? Both physically and emotionally."

"Women stay with abusive partners for years before leaving them," Lucas said.

"True. I wouldn't."

"You can't know that. Anyway, that's why I'm here. If I'd stayed at home the next time he saw me he'd have said something, promised me another thing, and I'd have gone right back to him again."

"Promise me you'll call Blond Guy." It was a statement not a question. Marie narrowed her eyes to slits and stared at him. "Even if it's just for work. You never know what might come from that."

"Tomorrow." Lucas walked to the balcony and leant on the rail, staring at the town below, wondering how many tomorrows he could spin through before actually doing what he knew he must.

The perfect anticipation must eventually end to give way to reality. A reality of another dancing job. A reality he hoped would be better than the one he had now. A reality that might just lead to love, dancing, and flourishing together in a relationship of equals, not of control.

All he could do was hope. For now.

But first he must make the call.

Chapter Three

A FEW WEEKS later, Christopher was in a restaurant writing notes for the review when his phone rang with a number he didn't recognise. He answered it. "Who is this?" He frowned and prepared himself for someone trying to sell something he didn't want or need.

"Is this Christopher? The Ikon manager gave me your number. I meant to call straight away but I thought I'd do it tomorrow. That was two weeks ago." The voice was soft, with a strong Spanish accent, pausing over some words.

"Who is this?" Christopher turned away from his laptop screen, straining to recognise the voice at the end of the phone. "Sorry, do I know you?"

"I wore the Superman costume at Ikon. The club." The voice paused. "The manager said you might know of some dancing work."

Ah yes, the dancer. That was weeks ago, wasn't it? He'd filed the story, seen it published and been to at least another couple of club opening nights since then. Three weeks ago, at least. His unsubtle ruse with the manager came back to his memory.

Christopher smiled. "Lovely to hear from you."

A quiet voice replied, "Laugh at me if you want, but I thought we...shared a look. Had a connection that night. I laughed at myself when I looked in the mirror." A brief chuckle. "I looked better in the gold shorts... Most things look pretty good in tiny gold shorts. So, I wondered if you maybe wanted to, sometime, have a drink with me. Talk about dancing jobs. You've probably got a girlfriend. Sorry for wasting your time."

Christopher smiled to himself. "No girlfriend. Never." His pulse quickened as he noticed the singsong quality of the man's voice. They had shared a look, a moment, and the dancer felt it too.

"Do you want to have dinner, talk about other clubs you could dance in? If it plays music in Ibiza I've probably written a review about it." Tiny gold shorts. Laughter. He doesn't take himself too seriously, this could be fun.

"Maybe we could dance together too?" The voice was hesitant.

Christopher nodded and found himself smiling at the romantic lilting Spanish accent. It made him think of bull fights, and flamenco dancers and passionate lovers...and those tiny gold shorts again...dancing across the stage... involuntarily he nodded at the suggestion. "I don't even know your name."

"Lucas. My name's Lucas." He paused. "You didn't look like you were enjoying yourself that night? I noticed because you seemed lonely."

"Same people, same conversation." *I want new people and new conversations. And someone who'll humour and love me and will dance through life holding my hand.* He wiped the sweat from his palms on his trousers. Maybe he was getting a bit ahead of himself. The man's voice was affecting Christopher in ways he'd not expected.

"I left Madrid for similar reasons." Lucas let the words hang there with a world of emotions unsaid.

"Me too—from the UK." Swallowing his throat dry, Christopher wanted to lighten the conversation. "Do you know the island well?"

"I think so. I've come here with family since I was young."

"I'm looking for someone who can show me the real Ibiza—the places where tourists don't go. I want new experiences, not new things in my life." The well-paid powerful job in the city with the penthouse flat and sports car he'd left behind hadn't made him happy now he thought back to that time. Everything had all just been a way to numb the pain from the misery he felt at his job. More things had meant more money which had meant more work, which had eventually meant a breakdown.

Ibiza was his parachute out of the rat race and only then had Christopher seen what his ex, Dan felt for him. The constant digs as he'd started to learn about spirituality had been brushed aside as being gentle teasing and not significant, but when he was off sick from work and Dan had told him to snap out of it and get back to work because he was holding them back, stopping them enjoying the life they deserved, Christopher realised Dan only saw him as useful for two things: sex and money.

"People and experiences are more important than things. But I must say that because I don't have many things!" Lucas laughed quietly.

"I left most of mine in England." Christopher had taken a small suitcase of possessions when he'd left—photos from the happier times of the relationship, some jewellery his grandma had left him, and the letters his mum had sent him while he was at university—and simply bought the rest on arrival in Ibiza. "Do you want to make some new memories together? Are you free tomorrow?"

"As a bird! Is that the right expression?"

"It is." And Christopher's heart soared with hope that maybe, when he hadn't expected to find it, he'd met a man who was the exact opposite of his ex. In all the ways that Ibiza differed from the UK, this dancer, he tentatively hoped, would differ from Dan.

THE NEXT DAY, they were sitting on a blanket under a tree on the beach. Lucas wasn't sure what this meeting was—a date, an introduction, or just the precursor to another hookup, but since the blond journalist—Christopher he'd introduced himself as—had agreed to meet he thought he may as well give it a chance. With a large dose of hope.

Lucas explained the typically Ibizan foods he'd brought in Spanish. "This is *sofrit pages*, a casserole." Lucas handed Christopher a spoon.

He took a mouthful and the dark sauce spilt down his chin.

Wiping it off, Lucas stared into Christopher's eyes. "It's pork, lamb, and chicken with peppers, potatoes and whole garlic cloves. Nice?"

Christopher nodded and smiled. After finishing that, he asked, "What have you brought for dessert? If you'd told me I could have brought something."

"All in good time. First, we will lie in the sun and wait for the food to digest. Next, we will have *ensaimadas*, which is a sort of pastry, and to finish I've brought *flao*." Lucas removed them from his bag, laying them on the blanket.

"And what's that?" Christopher licked his lips.

Lucas wanted to stroke the man's neatly trimmed blond beard. Coughing, he said, "Cheesecake made with local herbs and honey."

"Did you make it?" Broad white toothed smile.

Warmth radiated through Lucas's stomach as the smile penetrated him. He noticed the blond hairs on Christopher's forearms, wanting to stroke them, to wrap himself in their embrace he continued to explain the food. "I made the sofrit pages, but the rest, I have bought."

They were on Lucas's favourite stretch of quiet beach, in Talamanca, away from the bars and restaurants and crowds of Ibiza Town. Lucas was pleased at how laidback Christopher had been at his suggestion of that beach. Lucas's suggestions had all been accepted. He told Christopher about his work as a dancer. "I worked in small clubs in Madrid, working my way up to the super clubs in Ibiza. I worked in Ikon, but it is not my sort of club." *Except that it has led me to you.*

"Why?"

"Superman. Skulls. He made me do things like this. I don't like it. But I needed to work. I took it. Really, I want somewhere bigger, grander, more"—he gestured wildly with his hands—"me!"

Christopher looked Lucas up and down with a smile. "I see."

"I believe I am here to follow my dream. I believe I left mainland Spain because I must. Because I had to. It was not a good time there. He was not a good time." Lucas looked away, the memory of his ex flashing through his mind—the promises broken, the accusations, the constant questioning about where he'd been, who he'd seen and why.

Lucas swallowed, concentrating on the man sitting in front of him not the ex he'd left behind. He'd expected some questions about how practical dancing really was as a career, as well as a few orders about where to meet and what to do. Fortunately, none of these were forthcoming from Christopher—instead an easy going acceptance of Lucas's suggestions and interest in his career and dreams.

Christopher smiled, looking him up and down. "You stand like a dancer. Is that a silly thing to say?"

Lucas stood, spreading his arms wide on either side of his body. "No."

"What an exciting career to have."

"I'm on a long road but I will get there." *With support.*

"With support," Christopher said.

Lucas nodded, a warm tingling excitement and feeling of hope flooded through his body. *This might be something. He might be something.*

There was a silence and the two men looked towards the sea and then back at the food on the picnic blanket.

Lucas held out a slice of the cheesecake. "Try this. Do you like sweets?"

Christopher frowned. "This isn't sweets."

"I mean, does your taste like things that are sweet? I don't know how you say in English?"

Christopher replied, in English, "We say, do you have a sweet tooth?" He pointed to his tooth.

Lucas laughed. "Just this one tooth is sweet?"

Christopher shrugged. "It's an expression." He bit into the cheesecake and nodded in appreciation.

"I want," Lucas said in Spanish now, "a club, somewhere bigger, somewhere more in tune with me, somewhere, you know."

"Gay?" Christopher asked, raising an eyebrow. "You can say it. It's not a dirty word. Not any more at least."

Lucas blinked slowly, then stared out to the horizon, remembering the taunts he'd had to endure while at school for being the only boy who had wanted to dance rather than play football, the priest who'd told him he would surely go to Hell and there was nothing he or the priest could do about it.

"I know, but it doesn't feel like that sometimes."

Christopher stroked Lucas's shoulder, pausing to squeeze his hand gently.

"You, with these reviews you're writing, can you help me get to the right clubs?" Lucas squeezed the hand right back, holding his breath with hope.

CHRISTOPHER WIPED HIS mouth of spicy tomato sauce from the *patatas bravas*, and leant towards Lucas, feeling himself somehow drawn to this exotic creature. He liked going along with Lucas's suggestions for where to meet and what to do today because he knew they came from a place of kindness and wanting to show him the best of the island. A place of sharing. A situation where they could meet as equals. "I've been to new restaurants and eaten worse than that." He rubbed his stomach in appreciation.

"Thanks." Lucas began packing away the food into the little backpack he'd brought it in. "I must get back for something."

"It was meant to be a compliment. I wanted to thank you. You made the patatas bravas, too, did you?"

Lucas nodded and continued loudly packing and collecting into his bag. "Mamà's recipe."

Christopher held Lucas's hands, stopping him from packing, and stared into his eyes. "What I meant was I get sent all over the island to review new swanky restaurants, with their silly serving ways—on wooden boards or grey slate, sometimes in an old flowerpot—and their tiny little veggies and little swirls of sauce like a comma, and maybe a hint of meat—and all I can think is why? Why make it so complicated, so...self-conscious. Why not just serve good food done well?"

"Now, I understand, thank you." Lucas smiled as he zipped up the backpack.

"I want to see the real Ibiza, not the one they put on for holiday makers and reviewers—the one that's away from tourists and super clubs and review websites. Where is it? Cos I can't find it." Christopher sighed at the thought of the bar and restaurant reviews he had lined up later that week. Part of him knew he could write the articles without even attending and he'd be about 80 percent accurate.

"It is there. It is all around us." Lucas gestured in a wide circle with his arms. "You have to look for it. I came here because it isn't like home. Mainland Spain is beautiful, passionate, but here it's more free, liberal, everyone is welcome and no one is a stranger here."

"I think it comes from being an island. Where I came from is an island too, but that makes it different in other ways. The UK seems to look inwards—but I think here, you look outwards, to the sea, the world beyond, but somehow separate from the rest of Europe."

"How?"

Christopher shook his head. He was babbling, which is what he did when he found someone attractive and became nervous. He always got carried away with himself, the nerves carrying him from thought to thought without a pause between them. This dancer, sat next to him on the beach, couldn't have been more different from his ex—another City banker just like he'd been. Two bankers together and look how that had turned out!

He felt a pull towards Lucas—something, he felt sure, had conspired for them both to be in that night club on that night, and to catch one another's eyes.

"What are you thinking?" Lucas lifted Christopher's chin slightly, leaning it towards him.

Christopher shook his head. "Nothing. Silly stuff. So, you want to know if I can," he paused, trying to think of the Spanish word, then continued in English, "wangle you into a better club?"

"What does this wangle mean? It sounds rude, I think."

Christopher explained in Spanish. "It means, to use my connections and do something for you. To help you, but using everything I have at my disposal."

"I see." Lucas nodded slowly. "Tell me about this silly stuff you were thinking. I am interested. I want to know."

Christopher explained that as part of the real Ibiza he wanted to see, he also wanted to get to know the spirituality of the island so many people talked about. "And I wonder if there was something...I don't know, the island has created the situation for us to meet." He shook his head and waved it away with his hands frantically. "I said it was stupid. Ignore me."

Lucas edged slightly closer to Christopher. "It isn't stupid. I think above us"—he looked to the sky—"has a plan, is watching over us, so the spirits or whatever you call them, are always there. And here." He pressed Christopher's hand to his smooth chest next to his heart.

Christopher held his hand on Lucas's chest. At the same time he felt his own beating too, beating quickly in the presence of this beautiful, talented man. "Do you know what I mean about the spiritual places on the island?" He held his breath in hope, drinking in every second of this moment, in the perfection of the splendid now he was experiencing.

Lucas nodded.

LUCAS EXPLAINED HE'D been brought up Catholic and his family were very religious and how at first that had made it hard for them to accept him. He didn't say the word gay, because, even though Christopher had told him it wasn't dirty or anything to be ashamed of, old habits die hard. "I have two brothers and two sisters. We are a big family. This is what I want." He laughed nervously, worried he'd just accidentally asked the cute British man to start a family with him. "Not now. I mean, in the future. One day." He waved into the distance. "Many years from now. Now is for fun, for laughing, for dancing, for living. For love." There, that felt like he'd rescued the situation.

"More than sex." Christopher smiled weakly, blinked, then turned away with a sigh. "Sorry, not that I don't like sex." He coughed.

"This is right. More than only sex." Lucas paused, thinking about what to say next carefully. "Don't be sorry for your feelings. They are what makes us *us*. What makes us different from machines. I think you should sit with your feelings, really experience them, not be ashamed. People shouldn't stop other people from being themselves." Lucas laughed at the memory of when he was in the middle of his last big breakup. "You should have seen me before I came here." He shook his head. "I was a mess. You wouldn't have looked twice at me then. I hardly looked at me twice!"

Christopher was staring at him, the sun behind his head giving the appearance he had a yellow halo. "Some people think they know who you should be more than you."

"Yes. But this is wrong." And then, because he couldn't stand this waiting, the not knowing if his feelings were reciprocated, Lucas leant forward and kissed Christopher. At first, a gentle kiss, then slowly opening his mouth to allow his tongue to explore this new mouth, to find out what this new man tasted of and to wonder if there could be more than just sex. If there could be the whole universe of other things that made up a relationship and whether he could enjoy them with this man.

Christopher's beard brushed against Lucas's face, sending a message to force its way to his groin, imagining the soft bristles brushing against his stomach, his navel, his...Lucas pulled back, shuffling away a few feet for fear of getting carried away. "Sorry," he gasped.

"Don't apologise. I was enjoying that. Don't be sorry for how you feel." Christopher winked and reached for Lucas's hand.

"I know a special place where the island will reveal itself to you slowly. And where we can dance." Lucas's breath was shaky as he tried to compose himself.

CHRISTOPHER SHUFFLED TOWARDS Lucas, resting his hands on Lucas's lap, stroking the tanned skin of Lucas's legs, noticing how few hairs there were, turning to focus to the deepest, darkest brown eyes he'd ever seen. Christopher imagined those beguiling eyes watching him through lowered lashes.

Christopher's throat suddenly felt dry and his pulse raced.

Christopher wanted more of Lucas in his life, but worried it might be simply lust and lack of human contact since moving to Ibiza. Had it really been more than twelve months since he'd had sex? Was it the attention he was craving or the man? Could it be both? He winced as he remembered the last time with his ex. The shouting, and the packing, and the shouting, and the flight, and then the small apartment he now called home.

Before he could delve deeper into that thought Christopher noticed that Lucas was standing. He held out his hand and said something about a walk.

"Along the beach?"

Slowly, Christopher got to his feet, crouching forwards for a few moments to disguise his straining hard-on. He reached for his bag on the ground, and then he took Lucas's hand and was led along the beach. Warmth and happiness flooded through his body as he held on tightly to Lucas's hand.

Lucas carried his flip flops in one hand and walked in the white breaking surf, holding Christopher's hand with the other.

At first Christopher kept his shoes on and walked along the dry sand but then Lucas suggested they swap places and that Christopher should take off his shoes to feel the sand and water. Lucas leant forward to steady Christopher as he removed his shoes. They walked in silence along the beach with their arms around each other's shoulders, the soft sand between their toes, the waves gently crashing around their feet. It was peaceful and Christopher didn't mind when Lucas slipped an arm around his shoulders.

Christopher's mind flashed back to Lucas leaning forward as he removed his shoes, wanting to lay soft kisses along his spine from neck to waist and then to stand behind him, pulling Lucas's body up towards his hairy chest, pulling his arse back towards his straining—

He shook the thought away and tried to practice the mindfulness he'd been learning about. He listened for the rustling of palm trees in the breeze; the gentle lapping of sea on the beach; the squelching of his feet in the wet sand; the feeling of the sand squeezing through his toes. He allowed himself to experience with all five senses, and focus on the moment he was in now, rather than remembering or imagining others.

Eventually they left the beach and walked a few streets away until they stood in front of a white block of flats.

"This is where I live," Lucas said. "I want to show you the view from the balcony. There, you can see where I am going to take us. The special place." He keyed in a code and opened the door, holding it ajar with his foot.

Christopher knew exactly what would happen if he got to see Lucas's special place; his cock had been demanding only one thing since their first electrifying kiss not long ago. "I...I'd love to see your place and the view, but..." It was all going too quickly for him.

Lucas stared deep into his eyes and held Christopher's hand, placing it on his heart. "I don't want to fuck. Just to show you the view." After a deep breath, he said, "I promise."

Shaking slightly, Christopher followed him into the building.

NORMALLY LUCAS WENT to the other guy's place, or sometimes ended up in toilets or in a back alley, pressed against the wall, his arms straining as the other man's thrusts pushed him towards the wall. He trusted Christopher to bring him back to his apartment. He also knew that if he pushed too hard, too fast, broke his promise, Christopher would run and he'd never see him again.

Christopher smiled weakly, his sweaty hand tightening around Lucas's as they waited for the lift.

How do you know the difference between lust and a spark?—he mused as the lift doors opened to reveal the upstairs neighbour, holding hands with his girlfriend.

A brief smile and nod of recognition from the neighbour was all it took for Lucas to remember that particular afternoon when the upstairs neighbour had been above him in another way. His arse had been sore for days afterwards, but what was worse was how his heart felt. Far worse than sore, his heart had been broken by the neighbour's promise to see him again, to become more than just one afternoon on the floor in the upstairs apartment.

When I trust someone I trust them and I want the spark to become more. Only, so often, his spark was one sided, and he was nothing more than a fuck call for the other man.

By now on his floor, Lucas said to Christopher, alone in the lift, "The view, it is worth the wait." *And the man, I hope is worth the wait too.*

"Yes," Christopher replied simply, wiping his obviously clammy hands on his shorts.

Holding Christopher's hand again, Lucas walked through his flat to the balcony with the view of the range of hills on the horizon. He pointed to the tallest one. "This is what I wanted to show you."

"Beautiful." Christopher leaned forwards, his arms to either side of Lucas, and gently they kissed.

Lucas stroked Christopher's hair and soft bristles of his beard. "You are beautiful," he said almost in a whisper, pulling back from a long passionate openmouthed kiss, taking in the stocky frame of the man, his biceps straining the arms of his T-shirt.

Shaking his head, Christopher said, "I'm not. Your eyes. I could get lost—"

Before he could finish the sentence, Lucas kissed his neck, face and then lips.

They remained on the balcony kissing one another for an indeterminate time that both felt like an instant and an hour, until finally Lucas said, "Do you want a coffee?"

Christopher, leaning forward slightly to disguise his enthusiasm, shook his head. "I'd love to stay but I've got work."

Lucas smiled and waved, slightly disappointed that he'd not persuaded Christopher to stay, but pleased he'd not gone beyond what he'd promised.

Turning from the doorway, Christopher returned, left one last soft kiss on Lucas's forehead and lips, then made for the door, making the sign for phone call. "I'll call soon." And he was gone.

His mother had told Lucas off for trusting too soon, even when he was a little boy. He would meet people at school and the next day invite them to play at his place only to be disappointed when they broke or stole his toys and didn't want to play like him.

"Next time, you wait until you know them better, and then they can come here," Mamá would tell him.

And Lucas would nod and agree and promise to be different next time, but when he sat next to some new child at lunchtime he'd find himself inviting them to his place. Lucas always wanted to believe in the good in people—in the kindness of people he didn't know and in the need to be helpful to strangers because they may be important in your future. That was what his parents had taught him, so now, he reasoned, he was simply sticking to that. Lucas held tightly to the belief that he and Christopher would have sex when it felt right for them both, in their own time.

He knew although he had wanted to have sex with Christopher, by delaying it, until they knew one another better and it looked more likely to be developing into something, it would be so much more special. The kindness and interest in his dancing dreams Lucas had felt from Christopher made him hopeful that the British man would want to see him flourish and dance through his own life. And that they'd fit together in bed as well as they did out of it too.

Chapter Four

THEY DISCUSSED GOING to the festival together as a second date, both enjoying the sound of the word "date" on their lips. And then they'd talked about wanting to share the food, the spirituality, the countryside of Ibiza together at the festival.

"And more?" Christopher's last words were met with an almost silent yes from Lucas as they talked about how turned on they had both been on Lucas's balcony and what they'd both done to relieve the tension alone afterwards, which made the phone sex they had following that so much more fun than being alone.

The Mindful Life Full Festival had become an annual part of the Ibiza calendar and brought together all the less commercial, more spiritual parts of the island in a package that tourists could find appealing. Plus, it all being in one place meant the tourists—who only usually had a week to play with—didn't have to waste days trying to track down numerous hidden spiritual hideaways, mountain yoga retreats or traditional restaurants, because all those things had been collected together at the festival.

Lucas followed handwritten signs for the event, driving up a windy road that became a track and eventually ended as a gravel path where he left the car, among hundreds of others, by the roadside and completed the journey on foot. He arrived at the entrance where an elderly woman in a tie dyed dress wearing a flower necklace checked his ticket on his phone—the contrast seemed a bit incongruous to Lucas, but he shrugged it off—and then he entered the fenced border of the festival. To one side, the mountain dropped off sharply to the coast with dark water beyond that. To the other side were the green hills and villages dotted amongst the island's interior.

Lucas breathed in the clean hilltop air deeply then noticed something more appetising—the distinctive smell of a barbecue and cooking meat and...*what was that, oh yes, onions.* He checked the time and Christopher was due to meet him by the entrance to the festival village's tents shortly. His stomach tensed and suddenly he had no appetite no matter how delicious the smells. These tents formed a semicircle at the perimeter fence farthest from the music stage and dance marquee in a vague attempt to give its occupants a chance for rest during the festival weekend. In Lucas's experience, the tents were used for anything but sleeping, but he hadn't told Christopher that. He'd simply promised to book two separate ones. Which, reluctantly, and in a perplexed confusion, Lucas had duly done. Not before calling his sister to ask her what she thought that meant.

"He likes you, you called him, he called you, he came to your balcony and you made out like teenagers and now he's going to the festival with you, what else?" she'd said with a slow exhale of breath because she knew Lucas couldn't see her shrug.

"He can't like me that much because, you know," Lucas had said.

"He rang you. Besides, did you find out why he came to Ibiza in the first place? Bet he's been hurt."

"I've been hurt. You've been hurt. We've all been hurt."

"I mean, boyfriend of ten years, lost it all, wanted to live in a tent in a field hurt?" Maria asked.

"Didn't ask him. It's hardly first date stuff, is it?"

"Don't rush. You may trust him but that doesn't mean he trusts you."

"Going now, wish me luck!"

"Good luck. Behave. Be good."

"No chance of that, but I'll be gentle."

"That's my brother!"

And the call had ended, and Lucas sort of understood where his sister had been coming from and agreed that his tendency to leap before thinking or looking had often landed him in sex and no-relationship-afterwards territory. But he knew with every fibre of his body that Christopher wasn't the fuck-and-go type. He knew that if he got this right, and the connection he felt was real, he only had to follow his sister's advice and Christopher would feel the same connection.

Now, Lucas stood by the entrance to the tents, waiting for Christopher, thinking about the ridiculous sleeping arrangements he'd been forced to book and really the only thing he wanted to do was lick Christopher's body and find out how much of it was covered in blond hair.

WARM RELIEF RUSHED through Christopher as he found Lucas in the crowd. He waved awkwardly. "Hi, sorry I'm a bit late, I got lost after the ticket barriers. I did a left and ended up in palm readings and fire juggling when where I really meant to go was right, past the main stage—who's on did you say? If I'd have gone that way it would have taken me here. Only, instead, I walked past this guy barbecuing two hundred sausages and not normal ones like we have at home, but with paprika, spices, and they were serving them in some special bread I'd not seen before. The onions nearly had me grabbing a handful from that huge dish they were frying in. How do they make them smell so good?" Christopher realised, too late, that he'd been gabbling and simply filling the silence with chatter about not much in particular. He instantly regretted it.

"Hi." Lucas kissed Christopher's lips.

The closeness sent a shudder of desire through Christopher's body and he regretted the separate tents sleeping request he'd given Lucas. His mouth was dry and his cock was suddenly hard.

"They fry them in pork fat." Lucas smiled.

"Who, what does?"

"The onions, that's what gives them that amazing smell. Want to get some, it's basically lunchtime."

Christopher checked his watch—10:30 a.m. "I'm not that hungry. Maybe later." His stomach tightened and he wiped the sweat from his hands on his shorts. Despite the delicious smells he'd never felt less hungry in his life.

Lucas took his hand, leading him to a small tent. "This is you. It's the last small one. You can leave your bag and stuff here, rather than carrying it all day. Come back here to clear your head, get some space from the noise and stuff over there." He pointed into the distance where noise from the pipes and guitars on the main stage filled the air.

Christopher carefully placed his bag in his tent then sat on the ground cross legged, desperately trying to find his centre, or his chi, or experience the moment and not worry about the future—he never could quite remember which. And it wasn't working anyway. "For fuck's sake!" He banged the ground with a clenched fist.

Lucas, now sitting next to him, said, "What's wrong? I told you, I don't mind. I was glad you called. And if you need me tonight, I'm there." He pointed to another small tent on the opposite side of the horse shoe curve.

From what he'd seen so far, this festival felt a bit more Pagan than he would have liked. Plus, this whole laidback blissed-out Ibiza vibe was proving really hard work to get into. Why couldn't he just relax and be, and go with the flow like so many others did? This wasn't his holiday. This was his home, his life. He'd chosen this, but why did it feel like a jacket two sizes too small?

"Shall I leave you to settle in?" Lucas started to stand.

"I'm..." Christopher reached to stop him from leaving.

Lucas pursed his lips and breathed deeply. "Tired? Hungry? Thirsty? Cold? Hot?"

Christopher shook his head. "None of those. I'm not very good at this." He hung his head.

"It's your first time here, what do you expect? I'll show you round. Did you download the app, so you can find out what's happening at any time?"

"I did. And when I looked at it, I started making a list of all the things I wanted to see, and then I divided up the two days into blocks of time and allocated time to each of the things the app was telling me I had to see, and then I worried if I'd done them in the right order, and so I scrapped that, and thought I'd do it based on location, so I'd work my way from one side of the festival to the other. But then I realised I didn't know how big it was, so how far I could cover in any given time—the map doesn't have a scale on it. So then I researched this hill and how big the camp was, and then..."

"And breathe." Lucas held his shoulders gently.

Christopher, for the first time in days, or so it felt, took a deep breath. "I'm not very good at this." He gestured around himself.

"I'm not really into camping myself, but it sort of goes with the festival so..." Lucas shrugged.

"No, I mean, fun. I'm not good with letting go and relaxing, having a good time. I sort of overthink it."

"Okay. We can work with that. Why?"

"When I lived in London my life was full-on busy, stressful, working sixteen hour days, socialising and working at the weekend, sleeping no more than six hours a night. It's who I am." He paused. "Was."

"Sounds like a big change, why come here? You must have known what it would be like."

"I didn't have much time to research Ibiza properly. I just stuck a pin in a map and came. Plus, when I knew I needed to leave it all behind, I wasn't really very well."

"Had you not been to Ibiza before you decided to live here?"

"Good question. You'd think so wouldn't you—me with my preparation and organisation. I'd heard about Ibiza from friends who'd holidayed here. I looked it up on the internet—liked the sound of how laidback and spiritual it was. So I packed a bag and left."

"Just like that?"

"Just like that. As I said, I wasn't well at the time and I'd had enough of my beliefs being mocked and never having time to do anything about them. One Saturday I was about to do some work and I started to cry."

"Sounds like new job time to me." Lucas laughed quietly, obviously trying to lighten the mood.

"New job, new home, new car, new life, and new—well, no boyfriend."

"Right." Lucas bit his lip. "How long had you been together?"

"Seven years. Dan," the name felt awkward saying it now, "he was great at first, we would compete against each other for better jobs, bigger cars, and then we got the huge penthouse near Tower Bridge—a grand a week it was costing us in rent. And the car loans and the partying and the working. It was like a conveyor belt passing me by and every few seconds I had to pick up a piece, fix it to the next piece, and then another piece would come along the belt. That morning I wanted the belt to stop."

"And did it?"

"More or less. Look, you don't want to hear about this, it's not great date conversation. If I were someone listening to this from me, I'd run away, and fast! So anyway, your tent is over there. What should we see first?"

"Right there. If you need me, I'll be there." Lucas stared deep into Christopher's eyes, holding his forearms gently. "And when you're awake I'll stick by you, show you around."

Christopher regretted what he'd just said. Knew it would mean he'd be unlikely to ever see this slender electrifying Spanish dancer ever again, but after keeping the secret from everyone since he'd arrived, he couldn't keep it to himself any longer. What he wanted now more than anything was to lie in his tent with Lucas holding him, calming his breathing, making him focus on the moment. He knew Lucas would be good at that.

DAN'S MOCKING OF Christopher's beliefs had become so bad that he used to call out titles of books Christopher was reading and say, "Why you wasting your time with that? Load of codswallop."

"Do you want to get out of the rat race?" Christopher had once asked Dan.

"No, why? I like being a rich rat. I love to race."

"I want to do something different. Banking is boring. I want to grow things, in the earth, do stuff with my hands."

"You've been reading too many of your silly self-help books. Besides, what's boring about banking and money?"

And there had ended another conversation where Christopher had asked for a lifeboat out of his life and instead had been thrown an anchor to drag him farther down into his stagnating pond.

It wasn't until the Saturday morning when Christopher had logged on to catch up on some work he'd promised his boss that he began to cry. Not loud sobs and snotty gasps, this had been silent tears rolling down his cheeks, collecting under his chin, then streaming down his neck to form a damp bib on his T-shirt. *Why am I doing this? What does this matter? I'm only doing this to buy the next thing which will anaesthetise me from the pain of my existence—a gold fountain pen, a new phone, a pair of designer trainers—but if I were growing salads I'd happily wear anything to feel the earth between my hands.*

Christopher had lifted the laptop from himself and placed it on the sofa. His hands were shaking and his throat was dry. "Dan!" he called, not sure what else to do but knowing he needed someone to hear his reasoning.

Dan appeared and noticing Christopher crouched on the floor in a shaking heap said, "I thought you were meant to be working."

"Can you take me to the hospital? I think I'm having a heart attack. I can't breathe. My heart is beating too fast. Look at me." He wiped the sweat from his brow. "I'm dripping."

Dan, to his credit, ran to check Christopher's forehead and concluding something wasn't right, rang for an ambulance.

At A&E, a doctor checked Christopher for temperature, heart rate, breathing, booked blood tests, did a scan of his heart and finally gave his verdict to a quieter Christopher: "Definitely not a heart attack." He explained about the hormones the body secretes into the blood stream when a heart attack happens, adding that the ECG scan of his heart had come back normal.

"So, what was it?" Christopher looked to Dan for reassurance.

"A panic attack." The doctor looked up from his folder of notes.

"It felt like my heart was about to jump out of my chest. I couldn't believe I was going to die doing work on a Saturday."

"You were never going to die. It just felt like you would. Definitely a panic attack."

"So what now?" Dan asked, looking worried. "Can he go back to work on Monday?"

"I'm signing you off for a week. Rest and recuperate. Think about what triggered it. I see from your notes from the triage nurse that you're a banker."

Christopher held up his hands defensively. "It wasn't my fault—the financial meltdown. I wasn't selling the bad debts to people who could never afford them. Honest."

The doctor smiled. "Stress. It builds up in the body until it can take no more, and then you have a safety valve to release it. Think about why it triggered. Think about making changes to avoid it happening."

Dan rolled his eyes. "Yeah, like that's ever gonna happen. What's he meant to do? Work in a shop folding jumpers? Like we could afford the drop in salary." He laughed, then turned to Christopher.

"I'll be back with a few forms to sign but your heart is fine. Safety valve. Think about it." He left behind the curtain.

"Come on, we've got afternoon drinks with my new colleague." Dan stood and slapped his hands on his thighs. "Reckon I can get her a bit drunk and steal her ideas—then dinner with the upstairs neighbours, and we're going to that VIP club this evening. And you'd better finish that work—your phone's been buzzing all day."

"No," Christopher had said simply.

"No what? Okay, I'll see my colleague, you don't really need to be there, but you've got to come to the VIP bar and dinner with upstairs, we had them round so it's our turn to eat at theirs. I'll grab a cab and you can finish that work while I'm out and meet up again for dinner. Now, where would I get a cab?" He started to walk away but Christopher stopped him, grabbing his arm.

"All of it. No. Rest and recuperation. I'm staying home. You can ring my boss; tell him I'm signed off. I don't want to get to forty and die from burnout. How many people at your bank suddenly disappear at forty?"

Dan shrugged. "Couple. Few. Some. Whatever, that's them, this is you. This is us. This is who we are, so we just get on with it and it'll all be fine. I'm okay."

"You never sleep more than four hours a night. You're constantly popping diet pills during the day and sleeping pills at night. You're basically doing a Judy Garland. Don't think I've not seen you."

"Prescription medication. All legal." Dan shrugged and raised his eyebrows.

"Prescribed to you?" Christopher raised an eyebrow, knowing full well the answer because he'd seen the names on the prescription.

"Your point is?"

"My point is: I'm not doing it. Any of it. This is my body sending a distress flare for me to make a change."

"Yeah right." Dan turned to face the curtain.

"I could die. Next time it may be a heart attack. What about that?"

"And so, what are you going to do, go and grow vegetables in a hippy commune somewhere?"

"Dunno, but whatever it is, I assumed you'd want to be with me."

"Yeah, right, read another one of your little self-help books and watch a few TED talks and before you know it, you'll be right back to where you are now. Look, I'm gonna sort us a cab. You do the paperwork. We've gotta motor. We've already wasted three hours in this stupid place."

"You're not listening to me. Things need to change."

"Not for me, they don't." Dan left the cubicle to organise the taxi.

Christopher had tried to have an adult conversation about his options, about how they were a partnership and they could manage on Dan's salary while he worked out what he wanted to do. But Dan had kept talking about not wanting to carry him and how once a banker always a banker, and how it shouldn't be called the rat race, maybe the dog race, because dogs had much better PR than rats.

And so, finally when they'd returned home, Christopher had said, "I need to not be *this* me to work out who the *new* me is, what the new me does with his life. Do you understand?"

"Oh, I understand all right, but I think it's self-indulgent free-loading bullshit," Dan spat.

Christopher had stood in the living room, glancing at his laptop where this long day had begun, unable to understand how this man—who he'd shared his life and money and bed with for seven years—could say that.

"I'm going to meet my colleague and then I'm picking up our new iPhones, remember, we pre-ordered them months ago?" Dan kissed Christopher. "Bit of time playing with our new toys and you'll be right as rain." And then he

left, slamming the front door in the way he always did that shook through the flat.

Christopher stared at the laptop and let out a loud howl as tears ran down his face. He threw a few things into a bag—photos, a notebook of ideas—and left the apartment, his boyfriend and his life to catch a plane where he knew he'd get the exact opposite to the rat race if his brief research could be relied upon, the island of Ibiza.

He could only imagine that later, when Dan returned with two box-fresh iPhones, he feverishly opened his and began playing with it for a while before noticing the note on the table that read: *keep my phone, don't worry about me, I'll be fine—away from this—Christopher*

NOW, AT THE festival, Christopher stared deep into Lucas's beautiful brown eyes, remembering their kiss on the balcony. Christopher had soon got used to living in a small apartment, not eating out much and thinking about money more than he had before, but what he hadn't realised would be so strong was how much he missed having someone to kiss, someone to hold, someone to love.

Not just someone. A special man. This special man.

Was this Spanish dancer his lifeboat? Or was he just a warm body to wake up next to after months of craving? Christopher didn't know and couldn't tell the difference anymore because he felt he was just as fucked up now as he'd been in the UK, but in a different way.

"And breathe," Lucas said slowly.

And Christopher did, allowing all the memories and all the stress to leave his body and float up into the cloudless blue sky. And somehow, gradually, he knew instinctively Lucas was someone who could be his equal, who could calm his inner anxieties through kindness.

They spent the day together at the festival, Lucas holding Christopher's hand throughout. Towards the end of the day, Lucas had been explaining the different food options available, walking past huge dishes of yellow rice and seafood filled paella, the barbecue of Spanish sausages and piles of cheeses.

"Do you know what? I feel a bit sick." Christopher clutched his stomach to emphasise the point. He heard voices around him followed by laughter. They were definitely enjoying the sight of the stupid light-haired British guy not knowing what to do or eat at the Ibiza music festival. "You get what you want and I'll just have some water." Christopher shook his head as the paella man offered him a ladle of food.

Chapter Five

ALTHOUGH LUCAS WAS starving and could easily have eaten portions of all three options alone, he couldn't bear seeing Christopher so uncomfortable, so on edge in this setting. "Plenty of time to eat later. Follow me and I'll show you something beautiful." He led Christopher to the edge of the festival to see the red, yellow, and gold sunset over the sea. There he sat Christopher on a rock and slipped in behind him so he could wrap his arms around Christopher's shaking body. Lucas kissed his neck and said, "Look at the sunset. Think of only the sunset. Imagine you are the sun slowly dipping into the water."

"It doesn't actually go—"

Lucas pressed his fingers on Christopher's lips. "No talking, no thinking, just being."

They sat on the rock, staring at the sky and the sun until it was dark and the floodlights of the festival cast dark shadows around them.

Lucas left, returning a few moments later with two small bowls of food. "I got you a bit of each. Think of it like tapas."

Christopher ate and leant backwards to the warmth of Lucas's body.

"Did I tell you I'm dancing later?"

Christopher shook his head.

"You could join me at the front of the stage. I can get you into the special enclosure as my guest."

"What do I have to do there? As your guest?" Christopher held the bowl of food without eating anything.

"Nothing, watch me, sing, dance, drink, enjoy yourself," Lucas said. "You can meet my friends too. I told them about the disappearing British man!"

"I feel like I should be making notes to write about this for *Ibiza Discovered.*"

"You can, but that's not why you're here. You're here to have fun. Maybe another time you'll write about me dancing." Lucas winked, then stroked Christopher's back which was now still, expanding gradually as Christopher breathed slowly. His back arched forward in a gentle curve. Lucas fought back the urge to nibble his ear and lick his neck and kiss his chin with its irresistible dusting of dark blond stubble that he'd been imagining rubbing over himself since they'd met at the tents enclosure.

CHRISTOPHER RUBBED HIS stomach in satisfaction at being almost full. Lucas had been feeding him mouthfuls between talking about the music he was going to dance to later on stage.

Lucas wiped a stray dribble of tomato sauce from Christopher's face, smiling at the rasping of his beard on his own hand.

Christopher looked away, embarrassed. "I must look a mess."

"You look beautiful. Even with the sauce." Lucas paused, smiling. "Especially with the sauce. Your beard is so sexy I just want to stroke it all day long." Kissing Christopher, Lucas pulled himself closer, so there was no space between their bodies, allowing his mouth to open and his tongue to explore inside the shy man's mouth. Stroking the beard, Lucas continued the kiss until after an indeterminate time that felt like an age, with a deep breath he pulled away, smiling.

Christopher shook his head, laughing nervously and adjusted himself in his shorts.

A while later, after holding hands and continuing to kiss in silence, they made their way, hand in hand, to the front of the stage where Lucas introduced him to a group of friends. Christopher immediately forgot all their names, but shook the men's hands and kissed the women's cheeks while nodding and trying to remember the right Spanish words for how he felt—nervous, excited, anxious. He finally settled on happy because it was easier to remember. "I'll do it," he said finally after considering Lucas's proposal for a while.

"What?"

"Near the stage with you." He puffed out his chest a little bit, proud of his newfound inner roar, realising now that he'd not been thinking about what he should be doing, how he should be behaving, he was actually starting to enjoy himself. "This is why I came here," he explained to Lucas. He gestured to the starry sky, the dark water, and the hills with little villages twinkling their lights all for him.

"I knew you'd enjoy it." Lucas kissed him, slipped his hand under Christopher's T-shirt and stroked his hairy stomach.

Although he enjoyed the sensual touch, the gentle pulling at his navel hairs, with Lucas he wanted it to be more than a rebound which was why he wanted them to take their time.

Christopher watched Lucas dancing on the main stage—he spun around, moved all four limbs in time with the booming base-thudding dance music and he found himself smiling. *That's the man who wanted to see me. And I'm the man who's letting go of my worries and how I usually feel and just dancing too.*

Christopher had been dancing with the crowd close by the front of the stage but he still felt a bit self conscious. Others were close enough to flash the odd smile and exchange a few words but Christopher had plenty of room to dance alone, or with Lucas's friends who were standing nearby. He thought back to how Lucas had brought and then fed him little bits of food—something Dan would have rather died than do—and an internal smile radiated from his chest, a lightness filling his whole body like being just a little bit tipsy from a glass and a half of wine. The perfect stage of drunkenness—that's what this felt like, he reasoned, even though he hadn't drunk anything tonight.

He meant something to Lucas for him to have done that. And, now Christopher thought about it, Lucas meant something to him too—quite what he wasn't yet sure.

The opening few notes of one of his favourite dance songs filled the air and he noticed himself nodding, humming, and then singing along with the music. And then he was bobbing from side to side and then his arms were flailing and his legs were jiggling up and down until, powerless to resist any longer, he let his body give in to the tune, to the beat, to the moment. He closed his eyes and danced in time with the music.

Opening his eyes, he saw Lucas dancing beautifully on stage, flanked by others, but his man stood at the front, nearest to where Christopher himself was now dancing.

This is what I was looking for. This is the way life's meant to be. This feeling, is what I missed back in London with Dan and the job and the piles of possessions I— He stopped his thoughts from running away with themselves and concentrated hard on the moment, the beautiful wonderful now he was living.

A while later Lucas took them to a high point to watch the sunrise because with all the dancing and eating and talking the night had ended and the next day was beginning.

They kissed and Lucas put Christopher's hand on his own smooth chest. Lucas pulled back from the kiss. "I've given this to you. I didn't think you'd call, but you did. I didn't think you'd be gay, but you were. I didn't really think you'd come here with me, but here you are. You continue to surprise me. I know we have separate tents but I want to be with you at night as well as the day. You think I only want to fuck with you, but I don't. I want to be close and hold onto you all night."

Christopher felt his heart quicken and his cock stiffen but at the same time he felt an anxious sickness rising from his stomach, up through his chest to his mouth where it stayed, like a ball, blocking his throat, stopping him from breathing. This was what he wanted, what he'd hoped for, so why was he feeling so anxious? Gasping for breath, Christopher said, "Yes...but I can't. I'll—"

Lucas grabbed his hands and pulled them to rest on his stomach. "Let us go to your tent and see if that calms you?"

Walking slowly after Lucas, Christopher was led to his tent, breathing in time with Lucas's calls of "in and out, and in and out, and in..." until they arrived at his tent.

Once inside, they lay facing one another, their feet by the entrance.

"Feeling better?" Lucas asked, stroking Christopher's hand.

Christopher nodded, noticing the sickness had made way for excitement at the warmth and the musky smell of this man he was in close proximity to. He knew there would have to be a time when he properly moved on from his ex. The connection he felt with Lucas was real and gave him the strength to go with what his body was telling him, instead of his head, and he kissed Lucas.

Gently opening his mouth, Christopher allowed the taste of Lucas to fill his senses, the smell, the feeling of his smooth face against his beard.

They kissed for what felt like an age, slowly inching closer until their chests touched along with their straining shorts. Involuntarily, Christopher found himself rubbing against Lucas, enjoying the delicious friction coursing through his body, radiating warmth from his groin.

A tear escaped his eye as he realised how long it had been since being with anyone except his ex. "I..." The words stuck in his throat. "I want to, but..."

"Slowly, I understand." Lucas nodded. "You want if I spoon you?"

Wordlessly, Christopher nodded and turned over so his back faced Lucas's chest, now both lying on their left sides.

Lucas put his hand around to stroke Christopher's hairy stomach where it remained for some time. Christopher pushed himself backwards onto the stiffness he felt through Lucas's shorts, enjoying the delicious gentle closeness of the moment.

When he could bear to wait no longer, Christopher gently guided Lucas's hand inside his shorts inside his underwear, gasping as the hand grabbed him, gently cupping his balls.

Reaching behind, Christopher felt the stiffness and snaked his hand inside Lucas's shorts to reciprocate and noted with pleasure, the gasp escaping Lucas's mouth.

A silent nod from Lucas was all it took for Christopher to respond that yes, he did want this, his heart, his body and his head wanted this.

Christopher quickened his pace in time with Lucas pulling on his cock. Soon they were panting and with an involuntary thrust into Lucas's hand, Christopher came in a spurt that hit the tent. He continued pulling on Lucas for a few more moments until, with a groan and a satisfied moan, Lucas came, leaving a dampness on Christopher's T-shirt.

They lay together for a while until Christopher said quietly, "Good job I brought a spare T-shirt!"

Lucas nodded, then wordlessly kissed Christopher as he turned to face him once again.

A FEW DAYS later, alone in his apartment, Lucas was talking to his parents to let them know how he was getting on in Ibiza, trying to pursue his dream of dancing for a living. "I'm running out of money," Lucas said. "I may have to return home."

"What did I say? I told you it was foolish to up and leave it all for your dream, but would you listen to me?" his mum asked.

"I'm not telling you for sympathy. I'm telling you because I'm telling you. You rang and I'm telling you what's happening in my life. At the moment, not very much dancing is happening, which means there's not very much buying of food and very little paying of rent, but these are things I can worry about tomorrow." He waved away the concept of the money worries like a bad smell.

"What happened to the Superman skulls club?" Mamá asked.

"I hated it. I came here to enjoy dancing not to feel it was a compromise. When I turned up there it shouted—compromise—at me." Lucas had debated this decision for a while until the manager had called him "a high-maintenance queer" so Lucas had squirted lemonade at him from the drinks pump and told him to stick his job. He didn't tell his mother this because he knew she'd worry more than necessary and be more upset than him about the comment. Lucas was used to it by now.

"What will you do?" The worry in his mother's voice was clear.

"Throw a party. A farewell party." Lucas stamped his feet on the floor. "Invite everyone I know, spend my emergency money on food and drink and decorations. Leave with a bang." He laughed to himself at the plan he'd just that second come up with. He wasn't going to leave with a whimper and his tail between his legs. He was going to leave with style. After his sudden exit from mainland Spain to escape his ex, he wanted to leave differently.

But now he considered leaving in style, he realised he didn't really want to flee so quickly, not since the night in the tent with Christopher.

Christopher.

He wanted to show the man they could be so much more than only sex. He hoped they could be forever.

Just as another thought came to him his mum interrupted with another question.

"We will go now; do you want to talk to your little sister? She longs to hear about your adventures but now, I think maybe she would be better not to hear about it."

As he tried to arrange the thought, he said, "Put her on." And give us some privacy. After greetings, Lucas asked Maria to walk to another room.

Safely over the other side of the house his sister asked what he'd been up to.

"I can't come home." Terror seized him.

"Of course you can. You come home. You save up again. You fly back. It's easy. Maybe I'll come with you next time."

"I can't come back because if I do, I know who will be there to see me—there to tell me how mistaken I was to leave, and who will be only too glad to take me back." *And Christopher.*

"I always thought Pedro and you made a good couple. Why did you split up?"

Because he stole all my money. Because he took my heart and stamped on it with his cheating. Because he was such a good liar and so convincing that even after being caught cheating twice I still took him back and believed his promise to change. "It was complicated. I have a simpler life out here. Out here I dance, I earn money, I pay rent, I dance some more. It is the life I want for myself. The life I had with Pedro was not this life. The life I had with Pedro was more his life than mine." He couldn't bear to tell his sister the full truth, just like he'd not told anyone, because he knew that saying it out loud would show him up for the stupid gullible idiot that he really was. "I can't come back. I may still throw the party—see if it drums up some work for me." *And Christopher.*

"What party, what work, what are you on about?"

Lucas explained and offered Maria a place if she visited any time.

"If you're sure you're staying, then I will come soon. I want to meet this British man you told me about."

"I'd like that." He smiled to himself at the memory of the tent.

"How's it going?" Maria asked, after a long silence.

"Well." He told her about the festival and how they'd ended up sharing a tent. His sister didn't need the details. She'd know what had happened.

"*Maravilloso!*"

It really was pretty *wonderful*, now that Lucas thought about it. "I don't want to talk too much about it or it will jinx it." He bit his lip briefly.

"I understand," Maria said quietly.

"But, he...understands my dream. It's why he came here too. I hope..." He didn't want to voice what he thought for fear of sounding stupidly romantic and over the top, but his sister knew that was his nature.

"Go on, say it. I won't laugh. Promise. I hear something in your voice."

He shook his head. "Eventually, I hope we can dance through our lives together."

"*Hermosa!*" She clapped.

Beautiful, yes, that was right, he thought. Feeding Christopher food and wiping his chin were some of the most intimate acts he'd done with a man in a long time. "I calm him." He considered it for a moment. "He excites me, but he also calms me too." Quietly now, he added, "We fit together." Memories of the spooning in the tent brought a smile to his face once again.

After a few moments, Maria said, "Then fit with him some more, my darling brother. Look, if you need money for rent, food, whatever, let me know and I will transfer some. I don't want you to come home before you've fulfilled your dream. Love you, you big messy brother."

His sister's generosity made Lucas cry. How lucky he was to have such a supportive generous family. If only he could someday be that family for Christopher too.

To fit together with Christopher.

LUCAS DECIDED THE thought of returning to Madrid and leaving Christopher right at the start of their relationship was not an option. Plus the hovering, ever present ex-boyfriend in Madrid still scared him, so he sold some belongings to pay the rent he owed and asked around for bar work, which soon resulted in him working a few nights a week in a bar in San Antonio.

A few weeks later, between customers at the bar, as he briefly checked his phone for messages, he debated sending one more casual yet thoughtful text to Christopher: *how are you today? When can we meet up? Tired, wish I could rest my head on your furry chest again. Fancy coming to the bar where I work? Another evening of kisses on my balcony?*

"Two beers please," a man leaning on the metal bar asked.

As he collected the glasses and filled them from the cool metal tap he realised how much he wanted to fit with Christopher. He knew how right it felt and how relaxed and loving Christopher was, yet had still had to remind himself not to rush or be too much. *He's only out of a long, long term relationship and that must be a big change,* he reminded himself. Snapping back to reality, he pushed the drinks towards the man and accepted the money.

In his break, halfway through the shift, he stood outside the bar, taking in the warm night air and crowds walking past laughing, shouting, all seeming to be having a wonderful time.

Between selling his things and the job at the bar, they'd gone on two casual dates. One in a busy bar in Ibiza Town where they'd soon moved on from small talk and were discussing what had brought them to Ibiza. Christopher told him about the lifestyle he'd left and how he wanted to live a simpler, less materialistic life. "And no more mocking of me." He'd cast his eyes down at that. Lucas had shaken his head and held his hand and said, "I think love should come from being equals in a relationship." A brief shudder of Pedro's control had coursed through his body soon replaced by the warm comfort of the here and now in the bar with Christopher. Ending with kisses in the doorway of a bar, electricity coursing through his body as Christopher nodded how much he wanted to see him again, Lucas had felt their hearts beating quickly as their chests touched. "I will wait," Lucas had said, leaving with a quick kiss on the lips that had been met with a mouthed thank-you from Christopher.

On the second date they had gone for dinner in a simple quiet restaurant Lucas had suggested, and after spending the evening where Christopher had asked why Lucas wanted to be a dancer and how he'd tried in Madrid, Lucas said, "Before, I was not allowed to be myself. I was told this was a stupid dream."

"It's a beautiful dream. When you love your work you stop working. It's a quote." Christopher laughed. "From someone."

"I like that." Lucas wrote it on a napkin.

"Your dream is important. You are important. You are beautiful. Don't let anyone tell you otherwise."

Afterwards they went to Lucas's apartment where Christopher told him there would be no more waiting, "You are in here." He touched his chest, which Lucas kissed, inching his way up from neck to face to lips. And they undressed each other one garment at a time, between kisses and nibbles all over each other's bodies. Until they fell onto the bed and made love to each other with their mouths and hands. Lucas had wanted to feel Christopher deep inside him but when he flashed the silver packet Christopher had simply shook his head and mouthed, "not yet," which Lucas had accepted and returned enthusiastically to their gentle lovemaking until they lay spooning, sweat dripping down their bodies, and fell into a deep contented sleep.

Now, Lucas's parents' home number flashed on his phone.

"We heard nothing," his mother began. "You ring and say you have no money and then nothing. I spoke to Maria and she said you needed money. Why didn't you tell us? We would send you money. We want you to succeed. We have told everyone back home about the son who has travelled to Ibiza to become a dancer. So you must become a dancer, yes?"

Lucas started to say he was a dancer before he'd left, that he'd always been a dancer since he was a little boy, just not professionally, but thought better of it and instead explained he was fine and didn't need any money because he'd sorted it for himself.

His mother gasped. "Please, tell me you have not become a manwhore? The shame. The guilt. Gay, we learned to accept. We know you will find yourself a nice Spanish man to look after you. My neighbour, she said Ibiza is full of people selling their bodies. The streets are wall to wall sex clubs and black rooms and bars and God only knows what else."

"Breathe. Have you finished?"

His mother confirmed she had but still seemed to be holding her breath. "How is your Ibiza life? I have told everyone how well you're doing, but I don't know. I hope it's true."

"I'm still aiming to do the dancing, so you can carry on telling everyone that. But a lot of the people I spoke to came to nothing. There's a lot of talk and not so much action."

"You could go back to where you were dancing before. That sounded like a good club."

"Artistic differences," was all Lucas replied, still not wanting to tell her the real reason why he'd left.

"How are you eating, where are you sleeping?"

"I'm working in a bar. I'm there now. It's good. It helps me meet people." Lucas, satisfied that he'd calmed his mother down, paused to catch the bar owner's eye to indicate he'd shortly be back from his break. "Have you seen or heard from Pedro?"

"You are better than him! I will not speak of that man. He is banned from our home. After what he did to you."

In all fairness, his mother didn't know exactly what Pedro had and hadn't done to Lucas, but as expected, she'd sided with her son after the breakup. She'd pieced together what had happened from friends and neighbours and their children.

Lucas didn't want to talk about Christopher because he wanted to keep it private, quiet and shared with chosen few. His feelings of love were so strong and swirled around his head most of the time he struggled to verbalise how he felt, even to Christopher, never mind his own mother. They were at the time when all they wanted to do was see one another, sleep with one another, love one another, and even though the words "I love you" had yet to be said, they filled their every moment together, hanging in the air between them.

So instead, now with his mother, he preferred to talk about the dreaded Pedro because he knew how passionate his mother was in defending himself against Pedro. And Pedro was a more distant pain and one that now he'd been experiencing something right with Christopher, he was sure he wouldn't fall back into if he returned to Madrid.

"I will not talk to that man when I see him. I told him he drove you away," his mother said.

"That's not quite true. You don't need to do that. He has his life, I have mine." He wanted to ask her for a hug. He wanted to tell her he felt more with Christopher already than he thought possible. He wanted to explain how beautiful that night at the festival on top of the hill had been, how he knew he'd found a connection with someone on a spiritual level—more than some list of attributes to be ticked off, more than a mirror image of himself, but someone who filled in his gaps, not quite his opposite, but a knife to his fork, a left shoe to his right. How he'd found someone who would let him flourish into the person he was always meant to become. How they were at the beginning of their own perfect dance together, both moving to complement one another's movements, dreams, aspirations. But because he knew how soppy it sounded and how jumbled it all felt, he made his excuses, told her he was very happy and very lucky, and said he had to get back to serving drinks and he'd call her if anything changed.

He sent a text containing only a row of kisses to Christopher and waited for the response.

Immediately a row of red hearts pinged back into his phone, ending with "your Christopher"

Chapter Six

"SO WHAT HAPPENED to the dancer?" Sally sipped her cocktail, and crossed her legs.

Christopher brushed the salt from the rim of his glass, then did the same. "This has been watered down. That's going in the review. Who opens a cocktail bar that can't make cocktails?" He made a note on his phone.

Sally checked her nails, then quickly surveyed the room. "You're not expecting him here, are you?"

Christopher tried another sip of his drink, then stood. "I'm going to ask them to make some that aren't on their menu—see how they fare." As he strode to the bar he caught Sally's voice.

"Don't think I've forgotten. I'll be sat here waiting for you with my question when you..."

He didn't hear the rest because now he stood at the bar and asked the topless barman—so obvious and tacky he always felt and would say so in his review—for a Negroni, a Sidecar and a Slow Screw Against the Wall.

The barman explained that he didn't understand and could Christopher tell him what went into each of the cocktails please.

Making another note about the service and the barman on his phone, Christopher did as asked. Okay, so now he was up close, he could see the attraction of having six topless barmen—one in every colour, one in every size, a mix of smooth and hairy—they really were trying to cater for everyone's taste in this bar. Except those who knew their cocktails.

The barman's tanned chest had a dusting of glitter across his pecs—another step too far, Christopher felt. But he couldn't deny feeling a stirring at the smooth tanned chest and brown eyed Spanish barman with the curl of chestnut hair in the middle of his forehead.

Lucas was cuter, definitely. He checked the last text from Lucas and treasured the row of kisses, sending a flutter to his heart and a dryness to his throat.

After drinking the first cocktail he'd ordered and chatting to the barman for a while, Christopher had established that: one) he was straight—he mentioned his girlfriend three times in one answer; two) he also danced in cages at night clubs in Ibiza and that had been why he'd got the topless barman job here, rather than his cocktail making skills and; three) these cocktails were very much watered down.

The barman—he'd told Christopher his name but he couldn't remember it—helped carry the cocktails over to Sally who was sitting legs crossed, pouting and pointing at her empty glass and shaking her head.

"Where have you been? And who is this gorgeous specimen?" Sally's face lit up.

"He's on your team, not mine." Christopher plonked himself next to Sally and helped himself to one of the three cocktails on the table.

Sally grabbed the barman's bare arm. "Are you doing table service?"

He carefully removed her hand. "I have a girlfriend."

"Wow! So that's a no then. Look, love, I've got a boyfriend, but there's no harm in looking, is there? I'd prepared myself for a no show tonight since the bar is gay

gay gay, and then you go tempting me with your low-slung jeans and your glittery chest and before I've even had a chance to talk you hit me with the girlfriend." She pointed to Christopher. "He's writing a review. Of this place. Of *you* probably. So be careful!"

He left, and Sally and Christopher tested the cocktails, swapping them between themselves a few times until they'd settled on the one they each preferred when they took a long slurp.

Finally, emboldened by two and a half cocktails of medium to strong consistency, Christopher slapped his hand on the table; the glasses clinked and one fell onto the floor with a smash.

Sally leant down to clear it up but Christopher stopped her and said, "I was scared."

"No need for that, honey. It's only glass." She waved to catch the attention of one of the topless barmen. "I'll get someone over to clear it up. Not to worry."

"No, I mean with the dancer." Christopher felt the emotion welling up inside himself. The alcohol and the memories were proving too much. "At the start."

"Right, we're back on him now?" Adjusting her position in the chair, she looked ready for an in depth issue based conversation she was so good at having.

"Yes." Christopher sipped his drink. "It's going well. Like really well. Like soppy texts and afternoons in bed well. I didn't want to tell you because I wanted to keep it..." He searched for the right word. "At the start it was fragile. Rebounding me, and his ex was...well, anyway maybe Pedro and Dan should get together. I think they'd be well suited."

Sally swapped her empty glass for one half full. "Sounds fabulous. So you're enjoying it?"

Christopher remembered the dates, the walks along the beach hand in hand, the laughter, how interested Lucas was in his reasons for creating a life in Ibiza, how beautiful Lucas's dreams were and how much he himself wanted to see the loud flamboyant Spanish dancer flourish in his life and their times together in bed. He nodded.

"So tell me." She leant forwards, her chin resting on her hands. "I don't get jealous. Not much anyway."

Christopher wobbled slightly, narrowing his eyes at her little joke. "I've never felt this happy. He gets me. He listens. He doesn't laugh at me or my dreams. And," Leaning closer to Sally now, in a conspiratorial manner, he continued, "He's amazing in bed." *Too amazing?*

"Cheers to that!" She clinked their glasses together, then narrowed her eyes. "I'm a teeny bit jealous. Happy for you. Ecstatic really. The honeymoon period is so..." Staring into the distance, she was clearly searching for the right word.

"Yeah, it is." And it seemed to be lasting longer than honey moon periods normally did.

And so, over the rest of the evening Christopher told her about their dates and eventually showed her the text message.

"He's in here." Christopher tapped his chest with his fist.

"And the problem is?" After a sigh, she said, "I wish I was there with Will. Not a very demonstrative man, is our Will. Not verbally anyway."

"Nothing. It's just, I didn't think I'd ever feel like this again."

As they talked about his wonderful relationship and who he thought would say I love you first, Christopher realised he wasn't sure if he'd ever be able to talk to anyone about how inadequate and nervous he felt when Lucas had indicated the silver packet in bed. He wanted to be one, to be together physically with this man, sometimes he even felt as if they shared so much because their hopes and dreams were so compatible.

But when he should have been feeling excited, turned on, panting with desire at the prospect of fucking Lucas, instead, all he felt was anxiety. Anxiety that his body wouldn't behave in a way to show Lucas how much he felt for him.

Chapter Seven

A FEW DAYS later, in a large tent on a mountainside with the sun setting on the horizon, Christopher lay next to Lucas with both a raging hard-on and a sick feeling in his stomach. *What if he wants to fuck? What if I can't fuck? Is it really eight years since I've fucked anyone else except Dan?*

Yes.

What if I've forgotten how to do it?

No, concentrate on the moment, on the now, and all will be fine. If not I can explain to him how— Maybe not, how much of a useless lover do I want him to think I am? Having to explain why I can't fuck him, what a useless boyfriend!

Lucas leant forward and kissed him, long and slow, with his mouth open and his hand resting on Christopher's face. "I have missed you."

It had been a few days since they'd seen each other but it felt like weeks to Christopher.

Lucas reached down and unzipped Christopher's trousers, releasing his hard cock into the warm air.

Christopher gasped at the coolness combined with the tight grip of Lucas's hands around his shaft. As he grabbed Lucas's shorts and pulled them down over his hips his mind flashed to all the five star hotels he and Dan had fucked in. Quickly, he shook that from his mind.

He pulled Lucas's cock from his underpants and mirrored the pulling motion Lucas was making with Christopher's.

Lucas nodded and quickened his pace, so Christopher copied, they breathed hot air between their mouths as they thrust in time into each other's hands.

After a while, signalling with his eyes, Lucas manoeuvred himself so he lay top to tail with Christopher and they took one another in their mouths, their heads gently bobbing up and down in time together.

Christopher loved the intimacy of this. How it made him feel so close to Lucas, how he could smell his lover's scent while pleasuring him, at the same time as feeling the waves of warm pleasure radiating from his own cock as he felt the soft licking and nibbling of Lucas's skilful mouth on his body.

Moving himself back so they lay facing one another, Lucas's eyes widened as he nodded. With one hard, long thrust into Christopher's slicked hands, he jerked and came in a white spurt all over Christopher's hairy stomach and pubes. This immediately sent Christopher over the edge and his whole body willed him to thrust, to fuck, to push as hard as he could into Lucas's tight slippery hands, where he finished in a white fountain up Lucas's smooth stomach.

Christopher pushed his body as close as possible to Lucas's, removing their hands from holding their cocks, so their semi-erections were sandwiched between their sticky stomachs, causing a delicious amount of lubricated friction. Christopher smiled.

"Good?" Lucas asked, a smile in his eyes.

Christopher nodded. "I love you." He meant it with his whole body, his whole heart.

"I love you too," Lucas replied, and he drew a line of kisses on Christopher's chest.

They lay face to face, with Lucas on top of Christopher, clinging tightly together for a while, gently dozing, the salty sweat smell mixed with the distinctive aroma of sperm.

All working well. Christopher kissed Lucas's forehead and drifted asleep, enjoying the weight of him, resting on his chest and settling deep inside his heart.

A FEW HOURS later Lucas woke and carefully climbed off the hairy mass of muscle that was Christopher's body. The sight of Christopher sleeping naked on his back gave Lucas an instant erection. Lucas wanted so much to feel Christopher thrusting inside him.

Crouching over Christopher as he still slept, Lucas nibbled and licked his way up from hairy inner thighs, to lick his balls, lapping at them then taking the slowly stiffening shaft in his mouth, teasing it with his tongue, right to the back of his throat as he gagged slightly. Gagging on cock almost made Lucas come as his straining shaft dripped pre-come while he rubbed it lightly on Christopher's leg.

Christopher woke and looked up and started to hold Lucas back from him. "Hello, boyf—"

Lucas stopped any more words by kissing him, a musky, salty cock-tasting kiss, then licked and nibbled his way down Christopher's hairy chest, stopping to bite and lick his nipples, then to his navel and belly button before once again, after a tantalising delay where Christopher tried to thrust into Lucas's hot wet mouth, taking him deep into his throat and swirling his tongue around like he was licking the tastiest ice cream.

"I'm gonna..." Christopher strained the words out as his back arched, pushing himself into Lucas's mouth.

Lucas immediately pulled his mouth off Christopher's cock and left it dripping with saliva, straining into the air, the tip shiny with its hardness and slick.

"Lay on your back, I want to do you," Christopher said, just about getting his breath as his cock softened slightly as he regained some control and moved away from the point of no return where Lucas had been keeping him hovering for the last half an hour.

Lucas shook his head, and with a smile, ran one hand through Christopher's chest hair, pausing to stroke the well-defined pec muscles while pulling at his own cock. "This is what I wanted in the tent. Do you want to taste me?"

Christopher nodded and soon his mouth was full with Lucas's cock, thrusting in and out as he sat astride Christopher's chest, still rubbing the hairy pecs with one hand.

Christopher's cock strained, as hard as it had ever been as he smelt the musky sweatiness of Lucas as his nose buried amongst the dark nest of pubes.

They continued in this way for a while, gradually increasing the pace.

Lucas showed Christopher what he wanted now by placing his hand beneath his balls, pressing on his prostate, then gently inserting one of Christopher's lubed fingers into his hole. Lucas edged himself backwards on Christopher's chest, until he reached behind himself and pushed Christopher's cock to where his finger had been. Lucas pushed himself back, enjoying the delicious stiffness pressing against his prostate and then his hole and then just as he was ready to feel Christopher's cock enter him, the cock softened. Lucas edged himself backwards again, but as soon as he reached the tip of Christopher's now soft cock it moved away once again.

"I want you to fuck me," Lucas said, for the avoidance of doubt.

Christopher shook his head.

"What?"

Christopher gently lifted Lucas off his chest and placed him on the bed next to him. "I don't have anything. Do you?"

Lucas jumped off the bed to search for his wallet. Frantically flicking through the sections he found nothing but credit cards and cash. No silver packets. But he *always* had one. Then he remembered the coffee turned to cocktails turned to needing a condom with that guy at the gay bar in San Antonio. That had been months ago, way before he'd met Christopher.

Lucas ached with his whole body to be fucked by Christopher. All he could think of was having Christopher's stiff cock deep inside him stabbing at his prostate, feeling the hairs of Christopher's chest tickling his balls as he bounced up and down on his chest.

"We don't need." Lucas started to climb back astride Christopher but was stopped by two firm hands grabbing his chest and replacing him on the bed.

"Plenty of time for that in the future when we have the necessaries. No condom, no fucking." Christopher made a finished sign with his hands and shrugged.

Realising he wasn't going to win this argument, and feeling very impressed at the restraint of this man, and how much Christopher obviously respected both their bodies, despite having a cock inches from being inside him, Lucas lay down next to Christopher and ran his hands through his hairy chest.

CHRISTOPHER RESUMED HIS normal breathing rate. He wanted to be one with Lucas and he knew how good it would feel without anything separating them, but he also knew what would follow: the weeks of anxiety, the tests, the worry, and he knew minutes after doing it he'd regret it. He had more respect for himself and for this beautiful Spanish man than that.

His performance anxiety had put the brakes on too, but he didn't want to explain that to Lucas, to anyone really.

The way Lucas stroked his chest and nipples now made Christopher's cock as hard as it had been before the worry had softened it.

Christopher reached down to grab Lucas's cock and pulled it in time with his chest movements, pleased at how quickly both his and Lucas's cocks swelled in excitement. Once he knew he was near he nodded and Lucas once again climbed across his chest, his cock bobbing inches from Christopher's face. With one hand, he pulled at Lucas's cock and the other he used to massage the magic spot just below Lucas's balls, near his hole.

Lucas moaned in delight, pushing himself against Christopher's massaging fingers and with one final push as his hole opened for the slicked fingers, Lucas came in a wide arc all up Christopher's chest, neck and narrowly missed his eyes.

"Oh God!" Lucas shivered as he pushed himself into Christopher's fingers, then lay flat on his chest in an exhausted sweaty heap.

Christopher, pleased with himself for making him come that far and that hard without even fucking him, closed his eyes and kissed Lucas's forehead. Christopher's cock slowly softened, dripping pre-come down its length.

They dozed like that for a while but Christopher couldn't settle because his balls ached from being so close yet not finishing. Without really thinking when he woke from his slumber he found himself popping an almost instant boner.

Lucas crouched over him, face near his crying-for-attention cock.

Christopher shook his head. He knew from past experience that once he'd come the last thing he'd want to do was eat more cock, so he wasn't about to make Lucas do something he knew he wouldn't enjoy. He shook his head and then positioned Lucas across his chest, so his balls and hole were visible. He put Lucas's hands on his erect nipples and encouraged him to tweak and play with them. This was the perfect visual and sensual stimulation and within a few deep thrusts into his own hand, Christopher had come in a long relief-filled spurt all up his chest and face. He pulled Lucas down to lay on him and enjoyed the feeling of relief and satisfaction through his whole body, especially his now soft cock.

A FEW DAYS later, Lucas had organised breakfast on a beach after a yoga session. "I start every day like this to keep me supple for dancing," he explained as they arrived on the white sand.

Christopher looked at the crowd of people on the sand practising their moves as a gentle breeze blew. "Worth a go, I suppose." Christopher shrugged.

"You said you wanted to be more calm. To be more centred. To feel things more." Lucas stood on one leg with the other bent, his foot flat against his leg and hands in a praying sign in front of his chest.

Christopher nodded, tried to copy Lucas's position and promptly fell over.

The yoga instructor, a small Asian man in an orange toga, seemed to float over the sand, his legs moved so imperceptibly as he walked to the front of the class with his back to the sea. After a brief introduction and welcome he began the first move, something about a child, or a dog, or similar.

Christopher tried to copy him. At first, he spent more time looking at the others to check if he was doing it right, but he soon concentrated on the instructor and the moves and forgot how he looked, whether he felt silly and simply felt the sand between his toes and the wind on his face.

After the yoga class, the others milled about chatting and Lucas approached Christopher.

"Breakfast is served." He pointed to a large rug on the sand a few steps away, covered in fruit, cheeses and bowls of cereal.

They sat at the edge of the blanket near a woman carrying a tray of tea and coffee.

Christopher lay back as his eyelids felt heavy. "I could do with a coffee."

Lucas waved to the passing lady and took two cortada coffees with steamed milk and condensed milk settled at the bottom. "This will help."

"Does it always make you want to sleep?" Christopher closed his eyes briefly.

"Don't fight it. Feel how it is and accept it."

"Old habits die hard." Christopher shrugged.

"Tell me why, when that's why you came here in the first place?"

Christopher had already explained about wanting to leave the rat race but couldn't put into words why he felt he always needed to be doing, forging onwards, rushing. "I wanted to get away from it all." There, that should do it. He brushed some sand from his shorts and took a bite from a slice of melon.

"Isn't that what a holiday's for?" Lucas stared deeply into Christopher's eyes.

Christopher nodded.

"What really happened?" Another soul-piercing stare. "I left Madrid because I knew if I didn't, I'd get back with Pedro."

"If he was that good why did you split up?"

"He wasn't good, he was bad. Bad for me, bad for him. Bad for us." After a pause Lucas said, "So bad that I left the country. Plus, after practising in small clubs in Madrid, coming here meant I had a better chance of getting dancing jobs. Or at least I thought..."

That was pretty big, Christopher reflected. Tit for tat, it was time for Christopher to share his tat now. "I sort of had an episode."

"Of a TV series?" Lucas frowned. "Is that the right word?"

"One meaning, yes." Christopher was replaying the events in his mind—the crying at his desk, the driving to an empty car park one day at work and screaming in his car and finally, the weeks and months of sleepless nights that had got so bad he used to dread bedtime and that final Saturday when he'd been working at home—and wondered where to start.

Lucas held Christopher's hand, stroking it gently. "Start at the beginning—when you're ready."

And so, Christopher quietly started with, "I had a breakdown. That's what the doctor called it. I didn't want to say the word. It was an episode. It was an altercation. It was just another stressful day."

"But it wasn't any of those things, was it?"

Christopher shook his head. He told this tanned athletic smooth-skinned Spanish man he'd known for a couple of months, and whom he loved more than he'd thought possible, more than he'd told his close friends in the UK.

"I cried. I emptied my desk into the bin. I cried some more. I don't remember it— I only know what happened from watching videos my colleagues made of the whole thing on their phones. Kind? Cruel? You decide."

"What did the videos show you?"

"Lots of crying. Lots of shouting. And then I sat on the floor hugging my legs to my chest and rocking forwards and backwards until they took me home." Christopher stared into the distance, allowing himself to focus on the horizon— a town or city far away. "Of course, I went back. To work. Dan went mad. Told me I had to return. He shouted at me— which was exactly what I needed!" He laughed because the only alternative was crying and he definitely didn't want to do that. "I lasted another fortnight at work and then it all went wrong one Saturday." He told Lucas about that busy Saturday with the urgent work.

"So you came here to find what you were looking for?" Lucas summarised.

"Problem is I don't know what that is. I don't know what I'm searching for and I don't know who I'm looking to become." Biting his lip, Christopher paused. "I think you're helping me find out who that is, though. All I know is I don't want to go back to how I was living before. The flat, the job, the car, the Dan—none of it made me happy."

"Are you happy now?" Lucas wiped a tear from Christopher's cheek.

Christopher nodded. "I am." He wiped his wet cheek with the back of his hand. "I really am. I'm just not used to all this"—he gestured around himself—"time, space, unknowns. I was not a man who played things by ear."

"You will learn. I promise you. It is basically how I live." Lucas stood. "Come, let us dance." Lucas showed Christopher a few dance moves which Christopher felt were like the yoga but just done quicker.

As Lucas stood behind him to show him the moves— muscle memory, he'd said—Christopher felt the smooth arms against his, the hard chest pressing against his back, and if he wasn't mistaken the start of an erection against his behind.

After a while standing on the beach copying Lucas's dance moves, Lucas thanked the yoga instructor and waiters and left the picnic blanket to find a secluded bit of beach behind a rock where they dozed in the shade for a while.

An indeterminate time later, Christopher suddenly sat upright. "What's the time?"

Lucas rolled over, rubbing his eyes and yawning. "Who cares?"

"No, but seriously, what's the time? I can't find my watch or phone. Where are they?" Panic rose through his chest as Christopher frantically patted his pockets and checked both wrists as if doing so would magically make his watch appear.

Lucas pulled him to the ground gently. "I took them. We don't do yoga while watching the clock."

Relief poured through him as he remembered. "Right, but what is the time because?" He searched for a reason he needed to know and failing that simply said, "I've gotta know."

"Come with me. My place is close." He led Christopher by the hand and in a few short moments they were outside Lucas's apartment building and then in his flat and naked on the sofa.

Afterwards, Christopher admitted to himself that playing things by ear could work out well and he kissed Lucas's forehead and told him how much he loved him as they lay on the sofa naked, their limbs entwined as they cuddled underneath a cool white sheet.

"This much," Christopher said, holding his hands apart.

Lucas put his on top and pulled them wider apart. "This much."

Chapter Eight

AS A THANK-YOU for the beach yoga breakfast, Christopher told Lucas to meet him outside his place for a secret trip.

After buzzing him inside—and a hello kiss, which led to a longer nice-to-see-you kiss and then a thank-you-for-the-surprise–even-though-I-don't-know-what-it-is blowjob in the kitchen and finishing with a you-make-me-so-horny wank while standing in the kitchen facing one another—they showered, dressed and walked to Christopher's car holding hands and laughing.

Christopher stopped next to his battered but functional ten-year-old red Seat Ibiza—an appropriate car for the island in his view. He closed his eyes and felt the sun's warmth on his face.

"I'll unlock your door once I'm in—central locking's broken." He sat in the car and leant across to release Lucas's door. "And the windows don't work if it rains. Air con is just a light on the dashboard but no actual cool air. I've meant to get it all fixed but my Spanish isn't good enough. And I'm worried I'll be taken for a ride, stupid British tourist."

"Does it stop and go?"

"Just about!" Christopher prayed and hoped as he turned the ignition key. The engine roared into life.

"That's all that matters." He waved into the air dismissively. "I'm in love with you, not your car. Besides, you're taking me for a ride. I don't want any Spanish men taking my Christopher for any rides." Lucas coughed. "Where we going?"

Christopher was relieved at how not bothered Lucas was about his battered car. He'd hoped that would be the case, but hearing the words filled him with even more love for the Spanish man sitting next to him.

Christopher smiled. "Surprise." As the car pulled away with a gentle shudder indicating the clutch was on its way out too according to the internet Christopher checked later that night, he thought today's treat was probably a bit extravagant.

Before moving to Ibiza, Christopher had never thought about money so often and in such depth. In fact, he'd never given it a second thought—handing over his credit card without even checking the bill, filling his trolley with things he barely needed never mind wanted, and even less had price-checked, safe in the knowledge that on the 25th of every month a big wodge of money would replace all he'd spent the month before. Now money arrived in dribs and drabs and he needed to make sure he covered his rent and food and other wildly extravagant luxuries like that.

AS THEY ARRIVED at the five-star spa hotel—a large white building surrounded by trees, a lawn and a fountain by the entrance—Lucas laughed.

"What?" Christopher asked.

"For someone who said he wanted to be less materialistic, this is an interesting surprise."

"Why?" Christopher frowned.

"It must have cost you."

"I wanted to treat you." Christopher wanted a relationship of equals, not of competition as he'd had before.

"Next time I will treat you." Lucas bounced out of the car and ran towards the entrance. "Somehow!"

Anyhow is fine with me.

LATER, THEY FLOATED in the infinity pool, which from the hotel patio gave the impression that the water disappeared as far as the horizon just like the sea.

The hour alternating between the sauna, steam room, and cold plunge pool was something Lucas could definitely get used to. "I don't know how I'll be able to match this. Sorry."

Christopher dismissed it with a wave. "Something simple, with you, will be perfect."

"I'm not having much luck with the dancing. The bar work is still there so I must not complain."

"I'll talk to the guy who runs *Ibiza Discovered* to see if he's heard of any jobs or anyone who needs dancers."

"I didn't tell you for that." But it hadn't been a bad conclusion anyway—Lucas decided.

As they lay face down on benches while receiving back massages, Lucas suddenly felt like he could get used to this.

AS THEY ARRIVED at Lucas's apartment, Christopher said, "Good surprise? If a bit OTT?"

"What does this mean?"

Christopher explained. "Five star! Next time it'll be in a tent in a field." Because it had been so much fun last time.

"Coming in?" Lucas licked his lips suggestively. "I saw you staring at me while we were swimming."

"No." Christopher looked away. "And you. When we were in the sauna you sat with your towel facing me so I saw everything."

"And you loved it." Lucas winked. "Come on."

"I'd better go. I'll give that guy from *Ibiza Discovered* a call. See if he's heard of anything." Christopher kissed Lucas goodbye, but the arms around his neck and his taste and his smell were too much to resist and soon they were naked on Lucas's bed.

Afterwards, spooning in bed together, Christopher stroked Lucas's smooth chest and kissed his neck. "I could stay like this forever, but I must go home."

Lucas shrugged and kissed Christopher's hand.

I'll stay for another fifteen minutes, and then I'll leave. Christopher settled back to sleep in the arms of his love.

THE NEXT DAY, in a bar overlooking the sea, Christopher was having coffee with DJ Sasha after his manager had put them in touch.

"I'm always looking for dancers for my sunset sessions." DJ Sasha flicked back her long black hair and lit a cigarette. "Or I know people who are."

"It's for my boyfriend. Is it a gay night club you have in mind?" Christopher thought it worth mentioning just in case.

DJ Sasha waved dismissively, her floaty white-sleeved dress fluttering in the light breeze. "Sex and sexuality is a nonissue here."

Christopher shrugged, thinking when was the last time sex was a non-issue? If you're having great sex, that's a great issue and if you're not having any sex, that in itself is an issue. And pretty much everything in between were issues too, based on past experience.

"Thought I'd check," he added simply.

"Gay, straight, bi, trans, everyone comes here. The clever big clubs market themselves as being all about the music, and everything else is secondary. Whether you're a man looking for a man or a woman looking for a man, or anything else, that's secondary to the music. You will see." She gave instructions for where Lucas would need to go for the session, finished her coffee, and left, waving a salute of goodbye with a final, "Adios."

Christopher texted Lucas the good news, threw some money into the tray with the bill, and sat back after a good morning's work well executed.

A FEW DAYS later, Lucas was finishing his dancing set at DJ Sasha's sunset gig on the beach. A raised platform housed DJ Sasha mixing on her two illuminated silver electronic decks as the revellers danced in a roped off area of the beach while the sun set behind them over the sea. Lucas was one of the dancers employed to stand on raised platforms above the crowd flanked by flames. There were half a dozen platforms scattered throughout the crowd, and at any one time, two dancers were performing. When not dancing, they sat and surveyed the crowds beneath them, sipping water and catching their breath.

Lucas wore a black leather harness crossed over his chest and a black leather posing pouch to accentuate his bum and package. Behind the harness, two white feathered wings fluttered in the gentle breeze as he danced. "Greek sun gods," Lucas had been told when handed the costume at the start of the night.

During one of his rest sessions he saw Christopher sitting in a VIP wooden box to one side of the DJ booth. He was making notes on his notepad while sipping a goldfish-bowl-sized blue stemmed glass used for gin and tonic.

Lucas tried a few times to catch his attention, waving, shouting, and then finally he texted him with instructions for where to look.

Christopher did as asked then waved up at Lucas.

CHRISTOPHER CLICKED HIS pen and folded the paper back into his bag. He had more than enough for the review. Enough to be able to tell the *Ibiza Discovered* people he'd been there for work. Sunset, dancers, Balearic vibes, etc. etc. He took his phone from his pocket as Lucas stood to resume dancing and filmed his boyfriend for the next couple of minutes.

The way Lucas clapped his hands and stomped his feet in time with the music's beats, the gentle wave and curling of his arms mimicking the wings, these were movements Christopher knew he had no chance of ever being able to copy. Pride radiated from his stomach, filling his chest and without thinking he tapped the shoulder of the journalist sat next to him. "That man is my boyfriend." He pointed at Lucas.

"Lucky you." She smiled and turned back to her Martini glass.

Yes, he reflected, he was lucky. Even if he'd never expected to fall for a dancer—an artistic, peripatetic, temperamental Spanish man—but somehow, it worked, they fitted together. Lucas couldn't possibly have been more different from Christopher's ex. Lucas made him feel like his life was worthwhile, his decisions were good ones, and the pair of them were equals. Lucas had never mocked

Christopher for any of his beliefs or dreams, and neither had Christopher for Lucas's. They both understood how that felt.

DJ SASCHA WAS in the middle of explaining to Lucas her plans for the winter season when only a couple of clubs stayed open. "I am trying to put together something for winter. Something for tourists who want to enjoy Ibiza but without the crowds. Still the same fun and atmosphere."

"What will it be?" Lucas asked, interested to know more but a bit worried that it would, like so much on the island, only amount to talk and never come to actuality.

Sascha put her red-nailed finger to her bright red lips for a moment. "I'm thinking something along the lines of monthly. For families too. During the daytime probably. Meet me on Thursday and we will discuss in more details. I've a lot to work out yet, but I know I want to work with people like you. Even in winter your dancing will give it the authentic summer vibe."

Christopher squeezed Lucas's hand.

Lucas was about to ask a few more questions to help make up his mind whether this idea had a future or not, when his phone rang—his sister Maria. He made his excuses and took the call away from the noise of the crowd and music.

"Mamá, she's in hospital," Maria said, the terror apparent in her voice.

"What happened? Is she okay?" A thousand thoughts rushed through Lucas's head about his mamá and what he could do.

"She collapsed. She's in hospital now. Having tests. Under observation they say. You don't need to come, but I wanted to tell you." The tone of her voice told Lucas she didn't mean it.

"I want to see her. What if..." He turned to Christopher and nodded to DJ Sascha.

DJ Sascha stood, her black cape billowed out behind her. "Do what you must. We will talk again." She disappeared into the crowd of the bar.

"What's wrong?" Christopher frowned.

"It's my mamá," Lucas replied. He returned to the call. "On my way." Lucas ended the call. "She is all right—under observations, Maria said. She told me I didn't need to come. She knows it's far for me. What will I tell Sascha?"

Christopher stood. "Never mind Sascha, I'm taking you to the airport."

"I'm hardly rolling in job offers. I need this to see me through winter. Mamá said she didn't expect to see me, not now I'm here. If I was still in Madrid then..."

"Never mind work; work will always be there but you only get one mum and this is yours. She's not well. You go see her. Jobs come and go."

AT THE AIRPORT, having collected his passport and packed a bag of essentials, Lucas had made up his mind—if he was going, and now he was because Christopher had convinced him he needed to—he was going to pay for himself.

The woman at the customer services desk tapped at the computer and told Lucas the price of a flight to Madrid leaving in two hours from Ibiza airport.

It was more than twice what he'd made at today's dancing, which was the first decent pay cheque he'd cashed in weeks. He handed over his credit card, his hand shaking—after all, that's why they're called credit cards, isn't it?

Christopher placed his hand and credit card over Lucas's. "I've got this."

The woman drummed her nails on the space bar, looking from one to the other credit card. "Which card am I taking payment from, sirs?"

Christopher handed his over and gently swept Lucas's away.

"Thank you," Lucas mouthed silently.

"Pay me back when you can. No rush. I'm not going anywhere." Christopher smiled and planted a gentle kiss on Lucas's forehead.

AT THE DEPARTURE gate they hugged. "I wish you could come with me. You'd meet Mamá. I've told her about you."

"Another time. Different circumstances. I will meet her."

"I wish I could stay with you." Lucas felt although he loved Christopher, the relationship was still quite fragile as they were spending almost all their spare time together, getting to know one another, so abandoning it now would be like leaving a young plant without water.

The woman at the departure gate announced final boarding for the flight and asked everyone to have their paperwork ready.

Lucas showed his and walked to the door that led to the stairs down to the plane. He turned at the door. "I will call. Every day."

Christopher waved. "Be with your family. I'll be here when you get back. Go!" He indicated for him to go then blew him a kiss.

AS HE WATCHED Lucas turn and walk through the door, down the steps, and disappear into the tunnel to the plane, Christopher knew he'd done the right thing. The money was what Lucas had focussed on, but this didn't bother Christopher. Money came and money went. It was like the flow of water as far as he was concerned. Even though he didn't have much of it, he still treated it as a means to an end rather than a goal in itself as he had done with Dan.

The last thing he wanted was for Lucas to feel as if he owed Christopher for the money. Owed him in any way to imbalance their relationship. The money was just that, and the relationship separate.

Although he'd spent so long avoiding relationships to avoid rebound issues, now he'd allowed himself to fall in love, the thought of being without the passionate, complicated, loving dancer for an unknown period of time felt almost too much to bear.

They had been spending most of their spare time together since meeting and the gap Lucas's absence would open up felt enormous.

Christopher bit back the pain and wiped his eyes of tears.

How could they plan their future together if they were apart? What had Christopher done with all his spare time before Lucas had danced into his life?

"I'm sorry, my personality is bigger than my body. I cannot help it," Lucas had said on their first date. His small body contained a firework of passion and energy which even on that first night Christopher had seen sparking out of him with his loud arguments, his defence of the ways of the island and the passion with which he described his family and beliefs.

That first night, standing on the chair and performing a flamenco dance after a jug of sangria and no apologies, Lucas had been all him, with no excuses and no holding back. Because they'd not met on the gay scene, and instead at the random night club opening, it had made it special. Special because on the gay scene they'd have met, fucked, and parted.

And now, they were deeply in love and well and truly thinking about their medium term future.

It'll only be a few days. He'll be back within the week. No different from if we had a busy week.

Slumping in a chair at the airport, Christopher had no desire to return to the beach, his apartment or his life.

Sally's name flashed on his phone. He paused for a moment's more reflection about the love he felt for Lucas, now that he was gone, before finally answering her video-call.

"I heard. He'll be back. Absence makes the heart—" she said, waving into the air dismissively.

"How'd you find out?"

"Ibiza, everyone knows everyone's business. You're allowed the journey back home to wallow and then no more."

He smiled to himself. "I didn't know how much I'd miss him until he actually left. Stupid, eh?"

"Not really. What's more stupid is you feeling sorry for yourself when he's got an ill mamá in hospital and he will soon be back. Perspective please."

"Indeed." He glanced at his bag with the notebook and pen from the review where hours ago he'd been sitting enjoying the view of Lucas dancing and being paid to be there and wondering if life could get any better.

"He is fine. From what I hear his mamá's gonna be fine too. Come home and we'll order a big pizza and some ice cream and pretend like it was when we were *both* single." She brushed her hands together dismissively.

"Are you single?" He paused, thinking back to the last time her on-off boyfriend, Will had dumped her.

"Now that, my love, is another story. And one I'm not prepared to go into now, thank you very much."

"Aren't I pathetic? Poor me...pour me another drink..."

"The car journey only. Then it's a no wallowing zone."

"On my way." After ending the call, he shuffled through his notes from the sunset beach party and decided when he got home he'd call his mum to check how she was then make a start on writing up the review. Anything to keep himself busy.

Chapter Nine

A FEW DAYS later, Christopher was walking along the beach in the moonlight. He'd planned on doing it with Lucas before he'd flown back to Madrid, but in a burst of independence, keeping himself busy in the absence of any word from Lucas and an attempt to practice spirituality and mindfulness, he decided to really experience the beach alone.

He allowed himself to truly experience the wet sand squashing between his toes, the cool water lapping over his feet, the rhythmic pounding of his steps on the ground, his breathing in and out. Every time his attention drifted to the departure gate and how much his heart ached to see Lucas, he brought it back to the present. At each foray into the frightening future of no Lucas with no Mamá and no relationship, he reminded himself that was only a thought, not anything concrete and that thoughts were stories we told ourselves to make sense of the here and now.

The stories he'd been telling himself about why Lucas hadn't replied to his messages had been hard to avoid too.

Despite saying he'd wait to hear, Christopher hadn't been able to leave it at that, so had launched a mini bombardment of messages at Lucas, asking how he was, how his mamá was, if he'd got there okay, whether he had any news...

All very unhelpful. Not very mindful. And even less attractive when he'd confessed to Sally afterwards and she'd said, "You are a loon, my love. A big mad scary obsessive loon. In the name of all that's good and holy. Leave. Him. Alone."

No news is good news, or so the saying went. In which case Christopher had a deluge of amazingly great news so he should be really happy.

But he wasn't.

He paused to sit on a rock with his feet on the sand, facing out to sea as the moon cast a pure white glow across the black water. Lucas could be sitting watching the very same moon. The thought gave him a small degree of comfort and connection. Then his phone rang.

Lucas's smiling picture filled the phone screen and as he answered he felt his shoulders relax and a vague unspecific warm contentment fill his stomach. "Hola!" Christopher said.

"I forgot my charger. My battery has been dead. I bought a new one and then I had all your messages come through. Many messages. But not too many. I knew you were thinking of me."

Christopher could hear the smile in Lucas's voice and smiled in return. Christopher knew the jumbled mass of words Lucas was saying were to make him feel better because he knew Christopher would have been panicking about the silence. Christopher's heart was near to bursting.

"Mamá is recovering. She is in the best place for that—hospital. She is shaky. They said she had a fainting episode. She blacked out but they don't know why. It could be..."

The pain and worry in Lucas's voice were felt by Christopher. He wanted to climb through the phone and give him a hug. *Why can't you email a kiss and hug to someone, bloody hell!*

"It may have been a heart attack. But we're, they're not sure. We're not calling it that, not in the family anyway. When you start to say heart attack, you have to tell insurance companies and it changes things. Her blood pressure was high. Stress, age, salt, they said!"

"How is she now? When you visited her?" Christopher wanted to hear something positive, give Lucas a chance to share some good news on the call.

"All she wanted to hear about was my plans and if I could look after myself. She asked after you too—my British boyfriend she said. She wants to meet you, as soon as she's better, she said."

"Boyfriend—it always makes me laugh now I'm mid-thirties." Christopher chuckled to himself.

"That is what we say. There is no *manfriend* in Spanish."

"Same in English, we say partner too, but it always makes me think of a business partner." He shrugged to himself.

After a few moments' pause, Lucas said, "I can't leave her yet. The doctors say she must not have any stresses or shocks for now."

Christopher felt his heart sink. The anticipation of seeing Lucas soon dissipated and he bit his lip.

"You'll be okay, won't you?"

Christopher nodded, then answered that he'd be fine, of course he would. "You must stay where you're needed." Hundreds of words hovered in his mind that he daren't voice. "I miss you," he said simply. "Take care of yourself." Christopher paused, swallowed, then said the words he'd wanted to voice out loud for so long, "I love you."

"Te amo. Besos."

Lucas's *I love you* and promise of kisses in response warmed Christopher's heart to its core.

They ended the call.

Even though once again Christopher was alone, sitting on the rock by the beach, bathed in bright moonlight, he had hope and love in his heart.

It was a full moon. He wondered if that had any significance with changing fortunes or maybe something linked to high tides. Sally had mentioned a while ago that she always timed cleaning the apartment to very loud nineties girl power pop music around either a full or a small moon because apparently it helped remove the dirt. He couldn't remember which way round she'd told him, but it had definitely been linked to the moon.

Were his emotions so all over the place thanks to the moon? Or maybe, it was more likely that he'd just found a man he wanted to share his life with and now he was missing him.

A FEW DAYS later, Sally had organised an adventure yellow boat tour from San Antonio for her and Christopher because despite his best attempts as mindfulness Christopher had been, in Sally's words, "A great big miserable mope," since Lucas's departure.

"I'm trying," he'd replied.

"Yes, you are, love," she said.

"I know how selfish it makes me. But I can't help it if I miss him, can I?"

"That, you can't help. But how you behave when you feel like that, you can change." She winked with a smile.

Now, the yellow boat tour had left the busy town of San Antonio behind and was skirting around the coast approaching a quiet deserted beach, only accessible by boat.

Christopher shaded his eyes from the hot sun. "What happens here?" He'd thought the boat tour would be all about the, well, boat tour. He'd not expected to actually have to get off and do anything.

"Wait and see," Sally replied.

The boat moored and the boat hand boy dropped anchor in the shallow harbour, lowered the side and held the passengers' hands as they stepped into the cool clear water.

Holding his flip-flops in his hand and relieved he'd worn shorts, Christopher stepped into the refreshingly cool water that came half way up his calves and followed the other passengers to the beach. "I'm starving," he said to Sally as she plunged into the water and dropped to her waist, soaking her flowers maxi print bikini with a shriek and a shudder.

"It's refreshing. It's exhilarating. Beats Margate, don't you think?" She submerged beneath the water then reappeared blowing water from her mouth and shaking her hair about.

It did, undeniably, beat grey, cold, Margate—where Christopher had spent many childhood holidays—in every aspect, but that didn't stop him feeling hungry since Sally had rushed them out of the apartment early that morning with only a black coffee inside their stomachs.

As they approached the beach, a crowd stood in a circle around a man handing out bottles of water. He explained they would drink the water, change into swimming costumes and then go back into the water until they were waist deep where they'd follow his yoga class.

"Water yoga?" Christopher said to Sally. "What's with this place and doing yoga everywhere except where nature intended it—in a gym, on a foam mat?"

Sally handed her water bottle to him. "Drink that, I think your brain is dehydrated. Your sense of fun has certainly shrunk." She shook her head in disbelief. "You're seriously telling me you'd rather do yoga in an old gym on a wooden floor with a rubber mat than on a beach or in the sea here?"

"It's cold." Christopher splashed it about with his hands for a few moments. "Okay, so it's not warm."

"It's not the Caribbean." Sally turned away, throwing her hands up in the air. "I give up."

"No, no. Sorry."

"And before you ask, yes there's food, but only after the water yoga. Happy? Can your stomach cope with the wait?"

"It can. I can. We will." Christopher, realising he needed to buck his ideas up and stop being such a massive bloody mope, finished his water then strode to the beach where he removed his shorts and T-shirt into a pile on some dry sand and stood in his blue swimming shorts.

Blue swimming shorts that Lucas had said made him look like an underwear model.

Christopher smiled at the memory and a vision of Lucas's smiling face flashed through his mind. He decided that although he couldn't stop missing Lucas, he could stop showing it so much.

Sally was by now kneeling in the water, splashing her shoulders. "Do you never shave your chest? Nice tiny shorts by the way." She looked Christopher up and down.

"Thanks." Looking down at his chest, he ran his hands through the hair. "Imagine shaving your legs only much hairier and with more sensitive skin."

Sally shuddered. "Fair comment."

"Besides, Lucas loves it like this. Says it's his favourite part of my body." He smiled at the memory of Lucas's head resting on his hairy chest. "Right, so, water yoga. Let's do this thing!"

"Good to have you back, Christopher!" She stuck her tongue out then smiled.

Maybe, just maybe this wasn't going to be so terrible after all.

AFTER FORTY-FIVE minutes of water yoga, they were sitting at tables and chairs on a beach, enjoying cold tapas that had been brought on the boat.

Christopher finished the last mouthful of gazpacho, cold tomato soup, and then dipped a mushroom in aioli—garlic mayonnaise. "I know that him not being here isn't about me and his feelings for me."

"He's at his sick mamá's bedside." Sally ate a mouthful of tomato and garlic salad.

"Mamá is fine now. He's staying there because he doesn't want her to have any big shocks, or it could make her have another turn."

"Turn, is that a medical term?" Sally offered Christopher her salad, and he swapped with his mushrooms. They continued eating for a few moments.

"Doesn't stop me missing him, though. There's only so far cybersex can go." He raised his eyebrows. "I love being and having a boyfriend again. I like putting another person's feelings first."

Sally smiled. "Bravo!"

"Ideally I'd have had more time single before Lucas, but..."

Sally was nodding sagely. "When love comes you've gotta grab it. Give it a chance."

"I did. I have. You're lucky you've seen me. If it was up to him we'd have done nothing but seeing each other and you wouldn't have seen me at all." He smirked through a mouthful of chorizo sausage and bread at the memory of their first few weeks.

She smirked back and threw a piece of bread his way. "Thinking about sex?"

Christopher shrugged. "He's so demonstrative, too, which I'm not used to. In public he wants to kiss me and hold hands, and cuddle. Gay people don't do that back home in the UK."

"When will you stop calling the UK home? Here is your home now."

"Home as in where I grew up. Ibiza is home now, but they're both home to me. When I went home last Christmas there I talk about Ibiza as home, and when I talk about the UK while here, it's home because it's what I'm used to. Anyway, as I was saying before I was rudely interrupted, we walked around the *supermercardo* holding hands. He fed me bits of cheese at the deli counter to see if I liked it. The cheese cutter man didn't even blink. Imagine doing that in Sainsbury's!"

"It's all because of Franco," Sally said simply.

"The cheese?" Christopher pushed his empty plates away and rubbed his stomach in satisfaction. "I'm putting on weight comfort eating since he left. I must make sure I've lost it all by the time he comes back."

"He'd love you whatever. Besides, men should have a bit of something to grab onto. Men need curves too, a bit of soft furnishing."

"That's what he says too." Christopher shrugged. "Life's for living. Food's for eating. Love's for making." He laughed at himself and reflected the wine with the meal must have gone to his head. He lifted his glass of red wine for a toast.

"Who are we toasting?" Sally asked.

"Franco! You were talking about Franco!" Christopher shouted.

Sally loudly ssssshhhhhed him, shaking her head in disapproval. "Don't mention him here. It's no joke. If he came back, they would all chop off his head."

Lowering his voice to a whisper, Christopher asked, "So we're not toasting Franco then?"

"We are not. Franco always let Ibiza be more liberal and laidback than mainland Spain. Because Franco was so strict and regimented, controlling everything, when he finally went, the Spanish people's reaction to this was to be *very liberal.* Let everyone do what they want and not worry. Gay, straight, bi, whatever, sexuality isn't an issue. Why should someone get angry about two men holding hands while they choose cheese after years of a dictator telling them what to do? Puts it in context, don't you think?" She rolled her eyes.

Christopher nodded. He'd not really considered it before but now it was all starting to make sense.

"And Ibiza, because it's a small island where everyone knows everyone, it's all about relationships. As long as they respect one another, no one cares if you're sleeping with men, women or both. Choose whichever sort of cheese makes you happy and eat it with pride." Sally eyed Christopher up carefully. "As in, the cheese is the person you love..."

"Yeah, I got that." He collected his thoughts. Banter with Sally didn't always allow that.

The boat boy had started to herd the passengers up from their meals, gesturing for them to wade back through the now waist deep water to the boat, as it bobbed up and down in the sea.

On the return leg of the journey, back to busy San Antonio, they sat quietly at the back of the boat, the cool spray of salty water against their arms and the warm sun on their faces.

Christopher closed his eyes, lost in his thoughts of love, freedom and the differences between the two islands he called home.

Thanking the boat boy, Christopher dropped a handful of Euros into his hand and wished him a wonderful day. The boat boy smiled and nodded.

He thanked Sally for the day and its distractions from missing Lucas.

They got into Christopher's car and started towards home.

"It's just hard to have someone who's so full on, wanting to be with me, so proud of our relationship in public, and now all that's gone."

"Not quite." Sally shook her head.

"What do you mean?"

"It's not gone. It's still there. Here." She indicated her heart. "It's just on pause. But Lucas is just not physically here. You know that really, don't you?"

Christopher nodded.

"Now, tell me when did Dan last kiss you in public, outside of Soho or a pride festival?"

Christopher thought through their years together, through the pride marches and parties and afternoons spent at Soho cafés together and then realised he couldn't remember one time when Dan had even held his hand outside except then. "But I didn't hold his hand either." He wasn't sure why he was making excuses for an ex-boyfriend who was neither here nor would ever find out they'd been talking about him. But now he thought of it the way Lucas behaved in public reflected what he did in private—in the bedroom.

The sex with Lucas after a few months surpassed anything he'd ever had during the seven years with his ex in all ways. Not just the acts themselves, but the communication during sex, the way Lucas talked to him in the middle of making love, and how it felt like almost a spiritual act between the two of them. Undeniably he felt a deep connection with Lucas even just lying in bed together, without sex, and the need for silver packets hadn't been mentioned again so his anxiety about that had passed. Between the two of them, Christopher and Lucas had an imaginative and varied sex life and it was as if Lucas sensed Christopher's anxiety in this area so hadn't pushed it.

This communication, emotion, imagination was unlike anything he'd felt with Dan and their paint by numbers sex, even when they'd been physically one.

"Just because he doesn't tell you five times a day that he misses you doesn't mean he's not feeling it too. So he's a bit all over the place. His mamá's in hospital, that's to be expected—"

"Plus," Christopher said, "he's very emotional and all over the place at the best of times."

"Love is sometimes the little things like seeing something you know the other person would love. Hearing a story you want to tell him later. Thinking about the other person. I'd rather a conversation about how I am feeling and a cup of coffee in bed every morning than flowers on Valentine's Day. It's not all romantic dinners and marathon sex sessions."

"Although that helps!" Christopher grinned. He thanked her once again for the day and the distraction and the advice. "Sorry if I've been a bit of a mope."

Sally shook her head. "You haven't been. Besides, you've done me a favour really, all this."

"This what?"

"You two, the love birds. The separation, the moping…"

"How come?"

"I've finally given up on Will."

By now, at their apartment, Christopher put his hand over his mouth. He was so wrapped up in his relationship, in his so-called problems that he'd completely forgotten that Sally had been dumped after she'd told him. "I'm so sorry. I should've. How are you? Why? What happened?"

"Honestly, it's fine. I'm fine. I'm relieved actually. Like how you told me you felt when you finally left Dan. I don't have to worry, to try, to put all my energy into making it work. I said to him that anything that was meant to be wouldn't be this difficult."

"What did he say?" He couldn't deny her logic.

"He shrugged and said I was probably right." She shrugged to emphasise her simple point.

"Just like that."

"Just, as they say, like that, my love. No fight, no pleading with me to take him back like always before. Nothing. Just a quiet agreement. He picked up a bag of his stuff from our place last week and I've not heard from him since."

"Oh my God. I'm such a terrible friend. When we get home we're opening wine and talking about it all."

Sally shook her head. "I don't want to. Nothing to discuss. You have helped."

"Right." Christopher didn't really believe her. "How then?"

"Hearing about and seeing you two together I realised I'd never had that with Will and if I hadn't by that point I probably never would. We were both just filling in time with each other. It was easier to stick together in this on-off thing we had, than finally admit it wasn't working and start afresh. How was I meant to meet someone else, someone right for me when I was still wasting my time on someone who was very definitely not right for me?"

"Good logic."

"I'm going to shower to wash off the salty water and I think you were going to see how Lucas is getting on." She left for the bathroom.

Christopher sent a message: *How's things? I'm sleeping in your T-shirt. Ha-ha!*

In truth, he'd been sleeping with Lucas's T-shirt since he'd left because the smell had comforted him, but only now did he feel able to admit it to Lucas, with a jokey aside thrown in.

Straight away a reply came back from Lucas: *Mamá home now. I will be home soon. I wondered where that T-shirt was! Are you missing your red polo shirt?*

He replied: *it needed a wash. You took it?*

Lucas messaged back: *that's why I packed it! You'd left it at mine.*

Christopher called and began telling him the little details of his day, and Lucas did the same about what he'd done at his parents' home, right down to the breakfast he'd enjoyed of Nutella and toast with *café leche e leche*—coffee with two types of milk.

Christopher listened in contented silence as Lucas chatted away in a mixture of Spanish and English until they were both too tired for anything more than a kiss and an "I love you" in Spanish and English before ending the call.

Christopher knew all would be well.

Chapter Ten

THE CROWD WAS dancing in front of Sally and Christopher as they drank and tried to talk above the booming music. Sally had organised for them to have a small VIP seating and dancing area at Space, one of the island's largest night clubs.

A woman dressed in a black crisscrossed leather dress, only just covering her breasts and bottom, glided into their area to top up the ice bucket, remove empty glasses and replace them with new bottles of Coke. She lifted the small bottle of Grey Goose vodka Sally had needed to buy to secure her place in the VIP area. The woman's look was both disappointed that they'd only consumed a third and disapproving that there were only two of them to serve.

Sally smiled, indicated to her and Christopher and waved for the bondage serving lady to disappear.

With a swish of her long black ponytail she cantered off into the distance, checking others' drinks tables on the way back to the staff-only bar.

"We should do this more often," Sally said, pulling Christopher to his feet and encouraging him to dance.

He shimmied half-heartedly and put the glass back on the low drinks table, immediately messing up the serving woman's handiwork.

"Do you suppose they're given those dresses as uniforms, or do they all happen to go shopping at the same taste-free bondage dress shop?"

Christopher had been in a great mood since the last few calls with Lucas, but when he'd asked when he thought he'd be back and Lucas hadn't been able to be any more specific than "as soon as possible", Christopher had once again felt his heart sink.

"Give me another, just vodka this time, on the rocks. I could do with something to fortify me before going onto the main dance floor." He knew he was probably taking missing Lucas a bit far, but he couldn't help how he felt. The constant not knowing when he would return made the distance and time between them feel even worse. It was like driving to a new place when you feel you're almost lost—that journey always felt longer than the comfortable journey home. Christopher knew he wanted to feel Lucas in his arms again. And soon.

"Why on earth would you want to slum it on the main dance floor? That's why I've paid an arm and a leg for this booth. So we don't need to brave it down there." Sally pointed into the distance where a sea of heads and waving arms stretched as far as could be seen. Barely a space between each person.

"I'll be back. Stay here." Christopher walked past red velvet ropes marking the edges of other VIP areas, past the staff only bar until he reached a long queue of people waiting for something. Something amazing, it must be. He craned his neck around the queue and saw four closed doors with a woman stood outside holding a dust pan and brush. "What's everyone waiting for?"

A woman nearest him, whose eyes were wide and who'd been making rhythmic movements with her hands in time with the music, replied, "Toilets."

Christopher had seen enough of this so-called VIP area so he explored the rest of the club. Eventually he made his way to the edge of the main dance floor and found a space to stand next to a large hairy man wearing a black harness across his chest and a thin man dancing on a raised platform in a pair of tight black underpants.

Before he knew what was happening he was sandwiched between the two men, the hairy bear behind and the other man in front. The vodka meant he shrugged it off and went with the flow. The loneliness and wanting not to be a big old mope about missing Lucas made him lean towards the thinner man and introduce himself with a friendly, "Hi, I'm Christopher."

He said something incomprehensible in Spanish, then established Christopher was English and repeated it. "I am Miguel." He held out his hand for Christopher to shake then handed over a large drink.

Christopher took a few glugs, the vodka burned the back of his throat even though it was mixed with plenty of ice.

They tried to chat above the music and Miguel bought Christopher another drink when he'd finished the first.

Then slowly, Miguel led Christopher to the dance floor, pushed himself closer to Christopher and wrapped his arms around his neck as they danced.

Christopher stiffened involuntarily at the closeness of the gyrating, dancing semi-naked man.

Miguel said something into his ear and Christopher simply nodded because he felt drunk and tired and couldn't be bothered to explain he'd not heard and could he repeat it for it to be something inconsequential like, "where do you live?"

Miguel poured a test tube of bright red liquid down Christopher's throat and some spilled down his neck in a sticky mess.

The music was reaching a crescendo and the bear pressed himself against Christopher's back. He felt the man's harness pressing against his spine and then noticed a hardness jabbing into his behind. This bear must really fancy him. Christopher shrugged off the compliment with a smile. At the same time Miguel moved closer until his chest touched Christopher's. He felt a wet kiss on his neck—that can't be Miguel, because he's here, it's... It must be Lucas's lips. He allowed himself to lean into the knowledge that they were Lucas's lips on his body.

The kissing continued as hands snaked their way around Christopher's chest and stroked his stomach, pulling him harder back onto the harness and the erection. Rather than worrying about what might happen, and going over what had happened before in situations like this, Christopher concentrated his whole brain on being mindful and really experiencing the moment. This moment with Lucas, who he'd missed so much. And the experience at the moment was pretty enjoyable as moments went, he felt.

Another tube of liquid appeared and was poured into Christopher's mouth. The hands—of Lucas he knew—on his stomach were joined by more and they were delving into the waistband of his jeans, loosening his flies and grabbing his now almost full erection as he pushed himself forwards towards those hands, simultaneously pushing his neck backwards onto the wet kisses. He thrust himself into Lucas's hands that were now down his trousers. A bottle of something was forced into his half open mouth and he swallowed without thinking.

That vodka Sally bought must be extra strong because I don't remember— He stopped his thoughts from venturing into the past or future and returned to the moment, to the now. Sally, where was she? *Who am I here with? Who is this person rolling my cock around in his hands—*

Hang on a minute!

Christopher opened his eyes and faced Miguel who had been kissing his neck. He now kissed Christopher deeply while still teasing and squeezing the end of Christopher's cock with one hand and his balls with the other.

This felt good. His brain could try to deny that, but his body knew better. But there was something wrong with this and he couldn't quite put his finger on it. What had happened to Lucas? Where had he disappeared to?

He wanted Lucas. Not this. He wanted to feel his smooth body against his. He wanted to enjoy his tongue licking the end of his cock like an ice cream. He— Christopher pulled back from the kiss, realising this wasn't Lucas. This was, who was it again?

His head swam, the room tilted to the side, a sickness rose in his stomach, filling his mouth. Christopher put his hands in front of his mouth to stop himself from being sick.

He grabbed the hands down his trousers, removed them from his cock, pushed himself back into his clothes as best he could, and ran off the edge of the dance floor, stumbling as he tried to button up his shirt and tuck his cock into his underwear without making too much of a fuss.

He staggered around the night club, feeling cheap, used and taken advantage of while trying to find his way back to Sally and their quiet, empty VIP booth. He stumbled up some stairs which took him back to the dance floor where he'd been—accosted, assaulted—maybe not quite, but it had been something.

He asked a barman for directions to the VIP area and only followed the first two steps, which took him to a corridor of people serving food and trays of drinks. With the last reserve of energy, he walked across a seating area to the bottom of the steps that led up to the VIP section and was met with a stern-faced bondage server woman pointing to his forearm.

"Sally, over there." He pointed to where he thought she'd be but the woman simply flicked her ponytail over her shoulder and shook her head.

Defeated by the night club, the alcohol and whatever else he'd had foisted on him, and the two men, he stepped onto the pavement outside the club near a queue of taxis. *This isn't where we came in? Where the fuck am I? Actually, where the fuck is Sally?*

He checked his phone to find sixteen missed calls from one number—Sally. Resting on a concrete bollard that separated the pavement from the row of taxis, he called her.

"Where are you?" Her voice sounded strained and worried.

"I don't know," he replied.

"What can you see?"

He described the taxis and what else he saw.

"Do you want to come back in or are you done?"

Struggling to get the words out, his hands shook. "I'm done. Sorry."

"On my way."

A few moments later, Sally arrived carrying her handbag in front of her chest. She hugged Christopher, waved for a taxi and told the driver where to go.

"What's with you clutching your bag?"

"It's got the rest of the bottle of vodka we paid for. I wasn't going to leave that in there, not for what I paid for it. I could've bought a small bar in the middle of the island for that!"

"And in your coat?" Christopher nodded to her brown fake fur coat.

Sally removed two bottles of Coke from one pocket and three bottles of tonic from the other.

"Nicely done."

"At these prices, they should have given the drinks their own taxi back to ours. Anyway, up here for thinking." She tapped her head. "And down here for dancing." She pointed to her feet. "Talking of which, where *were* you dancing? I looked all over the VIP area and couldn't find you."

Christopher folded his arms across his chest, a wave of cold shivering through his body. "Not good."

OVER VODKA AND tonics back at their apartment, Christopher told Sally what he remembered once he'd taken his position on the main dance floor.

"Rohipnol?" she asked, mouth wide open.

Christopher shook his head. "I wouldn't be here now if it was. But they did keep pouring drinks into me. Big glasses of vodka on the rocks. And those little test tubes of glowing green and pink stuff. Every time I opened my eyes there was another one and they gave it to me."

"And you took it?"

"Well, yeah, I did, but I didn't realise at the time what they were trying to do."

"The kissing on the neck and the grabbing of your penis, they weren't a clue in any way?" She shook her head, leant back and crossed her legs.

"I blame your vodka for that, as well as whatever else they had in the drinks." Christopher sighed, putting his head in his hands. "I was spiked in some way. Otherwise I wouldn't have done that. I genuinely believed it was Lucas kissing me. I...don't know how, but I did. I know it's a crap excuse. And I wouldn't forgive me for it. I don't know what else to say."

"Not so easy, you were perfectly okay when you left me. I was taking you out to take your mind off missing you know who. Not so you could cop off with someone else."

"I don't think I did. Or did I? I can't remember. There was kissing. From both guys. There was some fondling and what could be described as I suppose, heavy petting." He put his head in his hands. "Oh shit." An image of his shirt flapping open with Miguel licking his chest flashed through his mind. This was shortly joined by remembering the teasing of his cock. "Did I?"

"What?"

"On the dance floor! Please no."

"Did you what?"

Christopher reached into his underwear to feel for a sticky tell tale sign of what he feared had happened on the dance floor. Besides being a bit sweaty, nothing. "Phew." Relief washed through him.

"I see. If you don't mind." Sally eyed up his hand that was still inside his underwear.

He removed it and apologised. "They kissed me. I didn't kiss them. I mean I didn't kiss them back. It was like an out of body experience. I thought I was at home with Lucas until I worked out there were too many hands and lips on me and the music was too loud." He paused, putting his head in his hands again. "I wouldn't believe it if someone told me this story."

"So don't tell him?" She bit her lip.

"I couldn't do that. And I'm surprised you're suggesting it."

"Off the top of my head. What would I do?" After a pause where she was obviously thinking she continued, "Love, you've gotta tell him. If he can't handle the truth—and let's be honest, you didn't sleep with anyone, it was a bit of a grope and all one-sided from what you've said and you were definitely under the influence of something, even if it was only alcohol—then ask if he'd rather you lied."

Christopher started writing a message on his phone.

Sally grabbed it. "What the actual fuck are you doing?"

"Like you said."

"I didn't mean now. I meant after you've slept and rested. I can hardly see straight now and decisions made in this state of mind are rarely the right ones. In my experience." She took his phone away, then kissed her hand and patted it on his head. "It'll all look better in the morning after a good night's sleep. N'night." She left the room.

Christopher stared at himself in the mirror—red blotches around his neck and chest. Love bites. Those guys had given him love bites and he'd just stood there letting them do it on the dance floor. What a terrible night. What had they spiked him with?

THE FOLLOWING AFTERNOON, once Christopher had risen, washed and had a stern talk to his reflection of a pale version of himself in the mirror, he called Lucas.

"I will come home soon," Lucas answered the call with an upbeat tone, before Christopher had even managed to say hello and ask how he was.

"Can't wait," Christopher replied, pinching his thigh.

"Why can't I see you? I love to see you for our calls. We have the technology, let me see you so I can kiss you."

Normally, Christopher had enjoyed seeing his face and the kiss to the camera they would both do, eyes closed, on Lucas's insistence to pretend they were kissing one another. But today, conscious of the marks on his neck, Christopher had opted for a voice call.

But not now.

Lucas's face filled the screen as he waved for Christopher to move closer to his. They counted to three as was their usual method and approached the screen for a kiss. Once that was over Lucas turned the camera round to show his mamá, sitting on the sofa, hands folded in her lap with a coffee by her side. "Say hello to Mamá!" Lucas ordered with a smile.

Christopher responded and tried to cover his neck with the collar of his polo shirt.

"I have booked the flight for two days. Will you meet me at the airport?"

"Of course." He looked away for a moment. "If you still want me," he said quietly.

Lucas frowned and walked to a separate room. "What is wrong?"

"I need to tell you something. I thought about not telling you but that's lying by omission. Which is still lying. So here I am, telling you. What happened. As much as I can remember anyway." He paused. "Are you away from your mamá?"

"She's in the other room and she can't understand English. Tell me, I'm worried now."

So, slowly, Christopher explained the previous night at Space and the VIP area and how it had been intended to cheer him up, but not in the way it turned out. When he got to the part where he was sandwiched between the two men after having the test tubes of unidentified alcohol poured into him and some bottles of what he thought had been water, but he couldn't be sure, Christopher stopped.

After a silence that Christopher could have driven a truck through, Lucas began quietly, "This, it happens. Maybe they wanted to take you home to fuck with you.

Maybe they wanted to steal your wallet and phone. Maybe they wanted to play with you on the dance floor and move on to someone else." He shrugged. "Did you call the police, or club security?"

"I didn't think I needed to. They didn't steal anything. Except my dignity. I used to see people on the dance floor practically having sex and think what do they think they are doing. Now I know, they weren't thinking anything. They were just doing."

"Did you have sex on the dance floor?"

"Depends on your definition of sex."

"Kissing—no. They played with you, yes?"

"To my shame they did." Christopher hung his head. "But I thought it was you. I thought we were at home. My head was all over the place. I swear I thought it was you. And among the sickness and the room spinning I realised you don't have two mouths and four hands. And then I ran away. But it took a while for my head to catch up with my body. Sorry."

"You didn't fall in love with them?"

"No. 'Course not."

"You didn't take their numbers and see them after?"

"No, no! I ran away. As soon as I knew they weren't your hands and your soft lips. I ran."

"Then I think, this can be the last we talk about it." Lucas stared at Christopher. The serious expression on his face didn't suite his normal bubbly personality.

"They were working together. One was kissing and the other was giving me drinks. It must have been drugs too."

Lucas shrugged. "Yes. This is how some people behave. You got caught up in it. But that is in the past. Now you are all right. Most people, they are friendly in Ibiza. Some people they are too friendly. These people you have to watch out for. Especially if you are in a night club. Where was Sally?"

"I left her in the VIP area."

"So you were alone and English." He nodded. "This happens. But not when I am with you."

And that was the end of the matter. Christopher couldn't quite believe how pragmatic Lucas had been when he relayed the conversation to Sally later. She thought he'd been very practical and very male about the whole thing.

People make mistakes.

She had summed it up as: "Better to have your erection rubbed by some stranger never to see him again than have exchanged numbers with someone and end up conducting a secret affair afterwards."

"Yes." Christopher nodded. Minor physical mishap cheating while under the influence of substances unknown—was much less to worry about than emotional cheating.

Chapter Eleven

AFTER A HOT busy flight and a taxi from the airport to his flat, Lucas finally walked through the front door of his apartment. Christopher had waited to meet him at the airport but the flight was delayed so Christopher had to leave for work after an apologetic phone call.

Lucas had been looking forward to the big reunion, a passionate public display of their love in the Arrivals hall, but no. And when he received the call from Christopher to say he wasn't coming, Lucas felt relieved.

Relieved and not disappointed.

What was that about, he wondered.

He put his weekend bag on the floor. Having taken a few days' worth of clothes and then staying for almost three weeks meant most of the clothes had been worn almost to death. He emptied them into the washing machine and absentmindedly switched it on. He slumped onto the sofa and for the first time since leaving to be by his mamá's side, sat in silence. As he began to enjoy the sound of nothing, except the washing machine doing its thing, he felt sad. Sad that if his mamá relapsed, she'd still be a two-hour flight away. Sad that he'd done all he could, but really, because he wasn't a doctor or a nurse, it hadn't been very much—sitting by her bedside, reading from her favourite magazines about horoscopes and recipes she promised to make when better.

"You must live your life, not mine." Her voice echoed through his mind.

That was why, reluctantly, he'd returned to his home. Only, now he was here it didn't seem as important to have come back to without Christopher to greet him. Lucas had been looking forward to touching, kissing, physically loving Christopher again so now he was back home alone, the pull of missing Christopher felt stronger than from Madrid; here he didn't have his mamá to keep his mind occupied.

After making himself a coffee with condensed milk, he tipped a spoonful of sugar in, stirred, watching the liquid turn from black and white to a light brown. Then on the sofa once again, he scrolled through the contacts in his phone. *I'll throw a party! A welcome home, we all missed you party!*

"There are all different sorts of families in life," Mamá had said. "If you have found yours, you must hold onto it with both hands."

When he'd been telling her about Christopher and how they'd met, and what Christopher and he would do together Mamá had squeezed his cheek, just like his grandma used to. "I see this. It is beaming out of you. You must go back to be with him."

Now, he turned back to his phone, mid-texting a group of friends about the party and a message from Christopher arrived: *Are you home? I missed you. Meet me and I'll make it up to you. xCx*

Lucas called Christopher who apologised again and said he'd make up for the fact that he couldn't collect Lucas from the airport, as promised. He'd had to leave to review a restaurant deep in the countryside, away from the beaches and clubs the tourists frequented. "The hidden countryside far from the coast is called Ibiza profundo which means deep Ibiza—hidden gems of the island," Christopher explained to Lucas.

Lucas smiled and nodded at his own suggestion from a few weeks ago coming to fruition. "I feel flat." *And worried about seeing you.* "It is all over and now I am here washing my clothes, making my coffee and the dishwasher needs emptying but I haven't done it yet."

"Life goes on. Your mamá is well. That's all that matters."

"I'm organising a party." *Because I can't bear to empty the dishwasher and slip back to life as if nothing has changed.*

"Has the bar kept your job for you?"

Lucas waved dismissively in the air. "I will call tomorrow."

"Did you talk to any of your dancing friends when you were in Madrid?"

Oh yeah, he had said he'd try to catch up with some—on the off chance they had some leads for work—and to be sociable obviously. "No time."

"I'm in San Carlos tonight—reviewing a hippy music festival and the restaurant with the—"

"Post boxes inside? I know. I told you to review it. Many English people live in San Carlos. Big families, big vans, long hair and tie dyed clothes."

"Meet me there. We can talk about your plans for winter. I have some people who may want you to work for them."

"I'm not doing any more bar work. Especially not in winter. It is dead." He yawned, partly through boredom and partly through fatigue from the journey.

"No, dancing. This hippy festival said they want some traditional Spanish dancers too. No glow sticks and streamers, but you can do traditional, can't you?"

Lucas nodded, then remembered he was on the phone and said through a yawn, "Yes." Something beeped in the kitchen demanding his attention. "I see you tonight. I must go."

"I wanted to say," Christopher said.

"Yes?" Lucas stifled a yawn.

"I'm so sorry for what happened in the night club. It will never happen again."

"I know. I trust you. I love you." Lucas paused, the anxiety filling his stomach like a heavy bowling ball. Trust. "Don't worry about not picking me up from the airport." It staved off the worry for another few hours. Lucas bit his lip. "What is the English phrase about absence?"

"Absence makes the heart grow fonder."

Lucas repeated it slowly. "Can't wait to see you." The bowling ball rose up to his throat, restricting his words. "I love you." He ended the call and automatically stood to see to whichever of the white goods was making the most noise and requesting he take notice.

As he hung his clothes on the airer on the balcony he wondered why after the anticipation of coming home, of seeing Christopher, of getting back to his life, he felt so unimpressed, unenthusiastic and anxious to be back now.

He sat on the balcony, lit a cigarette and stared at his clothes hanging limply in the air, then turned to Talamanca and the white sandy beach beyond that.

What is wrong that I feel this flat? How come the whole time I was with Mamá I had a reason to get up and something to drive me forward? And now I'm home I'm anxious about meeting Christopher, when I should be feeling excited?

And then it hit him.

He hadn't told Christopher about meeting Pedro while he was back home.

IT HAD HAPPENED one night when Lucas went to the little bar near his parents' home. The first night after leaving the hospital he was relieved she was alive, but sad that she could hardly speak and seemed to be only half there. After an afternoon of holding her hand, talking to doctors and plastering a smile on his face, he'd needed a drink when he left the hospital.

Without really thinking, he walked left to the bar rather than right to his parents' front door. Having crossed his papa at the hospital for lunch, as he was leaving and Lucas was about to arrive, he didn't want a minute by minute interrogation of how Mamá had been during his own visit, so instead he sat by the bar and ordered a beer.

After two beers he found himself telling the barmaid—a friend of his sister Maria's—about that afternoon he said, "I don't think I can do this day after day, until she is better." He wiped his mouth with the back of his hand and indicated for another beer.

She listened and poured the beer and handed him a bowl of salty nuts which he ate greedily since that was the first time all day he'd felt hungry.

"She looks so small. She hardly talks. Mamá always talks."

The barmaid nodded in recognition—everyone in this neighbourhood knew Lucas's mamá and her legendary capacity to talk.

"When she slept, it looked like..." He couldn't allow himself that thought because then he'd cry and then he'd cry some more and at this point, at the start of her journey to recovery, he needed to be strong and crying in a bar after the first afternoon would not constitute being strong.

Two large hands covered his eyes, a familiar smell of sweat and CK One filled his nostrils. Despite the painful memories, his body was instantly aroused by the touch and smell combined. He turned and was greeted by the grinning face of the only person who could bring about both an instant erection and a feeling of dread at the same time.

Pedro kissed Lucas's cheeks, brushing his week of beard growth against Lucas's neck, making him shudder at the memory of how he used to do that during sex. During the good, hot, toe curling sex. And then the memory of the control, the forcing, and tantrums returned, accompanied by a sickness, filling his stomach.

Lucas pushed him away and shook hands. Keeping him at arm's length was a good idea.

"Someone said you were back. Run out of money did you?" Pedro settled himself on the next stool, spreading his legs wide to reveal thick thighs, hairy legs beneath his dirty stained work shorts and a definite bulge at the groin.

Lucas felt sick and horny at the same time, in equal measure—the same way he always felt in Pedro's company. "Mamá is sick." Lucas busied himself with rolling a cigarette.

Pedro raised his eyebrows and offered Lucas one of his.

He waved the packet away and returned to staring at his hands, the rolling papers and the tobacco.

"You want to play?"

Back when they'd been together that meant only one thing. Although Lucas was a bit drunk, he was still in control of all his faculties and despite the earlier blip, all he felt for Pedro, now that he considered it properly rather than as a cock-jerk reaction, was pity and revulsion.

Pedro jumped from his stool and stood next to Lucas, his hot breath on Lucas's neck and the distinct odour filling his nose. He put his right hand on the bar. "We wrestle. Like friends!" He laughed loudly. "Unless you want to have a drink at my place." He jangled the keys in his pocket suggestively, deliberately pushing his groin towards Lucas.

"I just want to drink." Lucas pushed Pedro's arm away along the bar.

"Liar." Pedro stared into his eyes then grabbed his hand and pressed it into his groin.

Lucas pulled his hand away, shaking his head. "Why does it always come back to you? This isn't about you. It's about Mamá. It's about me. It's even a little bit about Christopher. But it's not about you. Not anymore."

"I heard you were trying an English man." He laughed. "How is Mamá?"

"Like you care." Lucas turned away and shook his head.

Pedro gestured to the space between them. "I care. You think I don't, but I do. I always did. When we were together, I did."

"Funny way of showing it." He shuddered at the memory. "Actually I'm going. Papá will be waiting for me. He'll want to talk about who's seeing Mamá during her visiting hours tomorrow." *Why is the Lord testing me? Why is Pedro here when I should be concentrating on Mamá and Papá, and I haven't even told Christopher I've arrived okay yet.*

"Stay, have a drink with me. As friends." Pedro gestured to the barmaid for two beers and resumed his place at the stool next to Lucas.

"Friends? You don't know the meaning of the word. Friends don't do what you used to do to me. Friends don't behave like this."

"I'm trying." Pedro smiled but it didn't seem to reach his eyes. "Give me a chance."

"Why should I?" Lucas said. "After how you treated me."

"You left. No note. You could have been dead."

Was this really happening? Was Pedro again, rewriting history to favour himself? "I left because you threw me out. Because you said you didn't love me anymore."

Pedro shook his head. "You misunderstood."

This should be good; how did I misunderstand? "Right." Lucas narrowed his eyes in anticipation of Pedro's story.

The barmaid nodded to check he was okay and he nodded back almost imperceptibly.

"I didn't love you anymore," Pedro said, "because you made me angry so often. You tested me. Who do you think made me explode like that? It wasn't me, it was you. Normally I am a calm, quiet man, but you, you drove me to the anger." And on he went, explaining that Lucas had deserved to be treated that way, that if only he'd have agreed with everything Pedro had suggested, they would still be together.

Lucas let him talk until Pedro had no more to say and finally he said, "It's fortunate that I am no longer here to drive you to that. I wish you well." He shook Pedro's hand, left some money on the bar and left. And despite it sounding slightly sarcastic, Lucas had genuinely meant Pedro well.

When he was a few yards away, nearer his bed for the night and a quiet conversation with his papá about tomorrow's plans to visit Mamá, he felt his arm pull backwards and his body swung back suddenly.

"Come with me!" Pedro shouted.

"Leave me alone," Lucas shouted.

"You know you want to. I won't tell anyone if you don't. I've missed you." He stuck three fingers in Lucas's mouth.

Lucas pushed him away. "Fuck off! I'll call the police!"

Pedro wobbled from side to side for a moment, leering through narrow eyes at Lucas. "Come back and I'll make you scream like you used to."

"In pain! In terror!" Lucas's fingers were poised over the numbers to call the police. "If you don't leave, I'm calling the police."

By now a few people from the bar had spilled outside onto the pavement to see the source of the commotion. The barmaid shouted at Lucas asking if he was okay.

Pedro grabbed Lucas's forearms. "You *need* me back. You *want* me back. Come and I will show you how much I've missed you." He was kneeling now, pulling Lucas to the ground.

"I don't need you. I have a life without you. You dumping me did me a favour. I'd been staying with you because I didn't know what else to do. Now I know I can live without you. And even if I didn't have a boyfriend I'd still be happier single and lonely than tied to you."

Standing now, his face red, his mouth sneering with anger, Pedro said, "I supported you while you were dancing for nothing. You owe me."

"If that's what you think, then it shows me how little you know about love. And you don't miss me, you miss using me—for sex, as a punch bag, as your servant."

The barmaid ran to Lucas. "I've called the police. I thought he was going to hit you."

Lucas shrugged. "If he had, I'm used to it. He has no power over me now. I am free of him. I'm going to Mamá and Papá's." He walked away to his parents' home where a short while later the police arrived in response to a call about an altercation outside a nearby bar between two men and asked if he wanted to make a statement.

Lucas looked from the policeman to his papa. "I should have reported him before but now it doesn't matter."

"It does. He threatened you. Look at your arms, they're bruised," the policeman said.

"I forgive him. I don't want to spend any more time on him. Mamá is in hospital. She needs me. Pedro doesn't."

It had all become such a mess so very quickly and Lucas didn't know how to tell Christopher about it.

AS LUCAS ARRIVED that evening at the rural restaurant in the small village of San Carlos—a small white church with a tiled square, in the north of the island, far from the beaches and clubs and tourists of the south—the lump in his throat told him he should tell Christopher about seeing Pedro, but he didn't want to spend any more time on Pedro than the year they'd been together.

Now was time for forgiveness and giving his time to Christopher, who was his present and future, rather than dwelling on his past.

Lucas stood on the edge of the road, searching for Christopher in the restaurant. A wall of post boxes on one side for the village's inhabitants and a disused phone box on the other, a dark wooden bar along the white back wall. As he stepped into the restaurant he saw Christopher at a table far into the building, sitting opposite a man. Both their elbows were resting on the table as they were deep in conversation. It looked intense and intimate.

Lucas felt a sickness rising within his stomach combined with anger and confusion. After the night club incident he thought it was happening again. Something similar. Something worse maybe. In confusion, his own guilt and anxiety mixed with anger and tears in his eyes, Lucas turned and ran away, back to his scooter.

As Lucas sat on the scooter, pulling on his helmet, Christopher arrived and held his hands onto the handlebars.

Christopher caught his breath. "When did you get here?"

He flicked his eyes back to the restaurant. "Who is he?"

Christopher sighed. "He is the owner of the restaurant. He took pity on me sitting alone."

Lucas tried to remember the man's face but couldn't because he'd only caught a glimpse from afar. "I...I thought. After what happened in the night club." He shook his head.

"I knew you were more upset than you said."

Lucas wiped his eyes. "I...I was fine. But when I saw you earlier it all came back to me. I've missed you..." Taking a deep breath, he composed himself. "His papa has owned this restaurant for many years."

"Yes he has. I've not reviewed it before so he was pleased to have the publicity."

"I didn't mean to." Lucas removed his helmet and switched the scooter's engine off. He was still very sensitive and shaken from the memory of seeing Pedro in Madrid and how it would affect his relationship with Christopher. "I talk before I think." He wiped a tear from his cheek.

Christopher was kicking the dirt. He nodded and kissed Lucas's cheek. "Shall we go back to eat? The owner will be wondering why I've left."

Lucas agreed.

"I've had some bread and olives. I was waiting for you to arrive. I was explaining to the owner when you arrived. Before you ran out."

"Sorry about that. I saw red. I...Come on." Lucas took his hand and they walked back to the restaurant.

"Let's start again," Christopher said.

I wish I'd just blurted it out, like pulling a plaster off. Lucas composed himself, still aware of the ball of unsaid guilt floating about his chest.

THE OWNER FUSSED over Lucas, getting him a sizzling bowl of garlic butter and prawns, a row of breaded and fried mushrooms and to finish, a glass of *Herbas*, the local spirit infused with herbs from the countryside.

Lucas enjoyed watching the man fuss around them, making sure Christopher had all he needed, did he want to try another of the wines, what about the desserts? All the while Christopher was writing notes onto his pad.

"I wanted to stay in Madrid with Mamá," Lucas began, as they sipped the bitter medicinal tasting Herbas from shot glasses together. The aniseed flavour mixed with the strong alcohol and made his mouth sting.

Christopher's face fell. "Why?"

"Because she needed me. She still needs me. She said she loves having her children around her."

"Why did you come back here then?"

"I am her child. I always will be, whether I'm in my thirties or fifty-five. She knows I've wanted to live here and work in night clubs in Ibiza since I started to dance. She used to iron my shirts back stage before I went on. Even though I wasn't being paid, she still wanted me to look my best. She would polish my tap shoes until she could see her face in them. When I was travelling all over mainland Spain dancing to get experience and some paid work, she couldn't come with me so I travelled alone. She wanted to see me succeed. Just because she loves me and I love her doesn't mean I am tied to her."

"You could have gone back to dancing in mainland Spain," Christopher said.

"It would have been going backwards. Returning. I'd served my apprenticeship there. It was not my dream and why I moved here. I wanted to live the life of Ibiza and for that I have to work here. That is not possible if I am going back to the mainland every month. Why did you move here?"

"Same as you I think. I wanted to live where most people come on holiday. I wanted my life to feel like a holiday I suppose." He laughed at the sentiment.

"Why are you laughing? It is not a stupid idea. Why do you think many people leave mainland Spain for here every year?" *And to escape from Pedro.*

Christopher smiled.

"Serious. You are here. You're not in Madrid. If we are together we should do it properly. Together." Lucas held Christopher's hand on the table and they sat in silence for a while until the owner of the restaurant placed a tray of chocolate mints near their hands and left.

They made their way back to Lucas's apartment and had frantic desperate missing each other sex. They grabbed at each other's stiff, aching cocks after an evening of stroking legs under the table, until all too quickly they both came in long white ropes across the bedroom floor, for they hadn't even managed to make it to the bed.

Afterwards, they lay side by side sleeping until the early morning when Lucas woke with an erection jabbing into Christopher's back. He pushed it gently, while kissing Christopher's neck until he yawned and stretched and turned over to face Lucas.

"Have the love bites gone?" Lucas asked. "I know you told me about them and I promised it was forgotten but I don't like the marks of another on you."

"They've mostly gone," Christopher said, casting his eyes downwards.

Lucas shook his head then kissed Christopher's lips, opening his mouth. They kissed with open mouths and exploring tongues while the rest of their bodies woke up.

CHRISTOPHER RUBBED HIS stiff cock against Lucas's, slicked with his spit as their heads slid together in his hand. They remained like this as Christopher gathered pace with his fist until in a delicious moment of perfect unity they both came in a short spurt between their bodies at the same time.

Christopher's natural inclination was to jump out of bed and reach for something to clean up with but Lucas held onto him tightly with both hands around his waist, pushing them closer together so the stickiness spread over their stomachs and there they returned to sleep, facing one another, and breathing in the hot air between their faces.

THE FOLLOWING MORNING they lay in bed together spooning, Christopher pressed himself behind Lucas, gently kissing his neck to wake him. The warmth of Lucas's arse against him gave Christopher an erection. Christopher had waited for this moment for so long. His wallet had the required contents, but his heart was full of butterflies. Could he live up to what Lucas was expecting—what he was needing from him? Having not fucked another man since Dan, albeit infrequently, in eight years, Lucas's needs were a lot for Christopher to live up to.

They lay side by side, Christopher pressing his cock into Lucas's arse, kissing his neck. Rhythmically Christopher pulled on Lucas's erection in time with his own thrusts.

They were building in pace and suddenly the pleasure was almost ruined when, with a nod, Lucas pushed Christopher onto his back. He positioned himself astride Christopher's chest and said all he wanted and needed at that moment wordlessly by simply pressing Christopher's cock against his hole.

What if I go soft? What if I can't fuck hard enough? What if I fuck too hard and hurt him? Their lovemaking up to that point had been pretty slow, sensual, loving really, when Christopher thought about it. But Lucas had this point when he seemed to want things a bit harder, less gentle and more...fucking.

The view of Lucas astride him, his cock banging on Christopher's chest, turned him on so much he thought it would be over before he'd had time to reach for his wallet. He loved this man so much. He loved his body so much he wanted to climb inside him sometimes. That was how Lucas had described his need for this to Christopher when they'd talked about it before.

So, not much to live up to then?

Christopher looked away from the sight of his boyfriend waiting in anticipation to calm himself down and remove some of the build up he was now feeling for the event. *The event—that's definitely not a helpful term to use at this point.* He manoeuvred Lucas onto his right side and then positioned himself behind him once again. He smelt Lucas's neck and then kissed it. From here he could keep control of how turned on he felt. From this position he could do it as he wanted to be with Lucas—gently, gradually, carefully.

"I want...your chest..." Lucas's words strained from his mouth.

"I know. Later," Christopher replied. He knew how much Lucas loved his favourite position but couldn't start like that, so he thought he'd work up to it, maybe tonight, maybe the next time. *Just concentrate on now*, he told himself.

First Christopher slicked Lucas, still spooning him from behind, smelling his hair, his sweat, his body. Then he pulled the condom on, adding more slick.

Lucas gasped and mumbled some words about wanting to do that with his mouth.

"Next time," he replied simply while pushing the tip of his cock up to Lucas's hole. Reaching round the side with his hand he grabbed Lucas's cock and pulled down the shaft, cupping the tightened balls with his hand.

Lucas moaned and pushed himself backwards, as hoped, onto Christopher's slicked stiff cock.

Never a man to do things unprepared, as well as making sure he had the right accoutrements, Christopher had read up on top tips for this type of sex. They were so compatible in many other ways that he didn't want to be the boyfriend who was a terrible fuck.

Resisting with all his natural male urges to thrust deep into Lucas's arse, Christopher simply kissed his neck and stroked a few more times on Lucas's shaft.

Lucas once again edged himself backwards, lifting up his own legs to open himself to Christopher so that he began to enter.

Does he need more lube? Am I hurting him? Is he wanting me to hurt him? These thoughts, and hundreds more flashed around Christopher's head. He recalled the tips and simply remained still, knowing Lucas would proceed at the pace right for him and as long as Christopher himself resisted thrusting forward, and remained turned on, there would be no gasps of pain, no rushed fucking, only perfectly timed lovemaking.

Lucas pushed himself backwards gradually, opening to receive Christopher's stiffness like a knife through butter until after a few more shuffles backwards and some more teasing of his own now dripping, stiff cock, Lucas and Christopher were one.

They lay there for a few moments. Christopher enjoyed the warm tightness around his cock and when Lucas tightened *those* muscles, his eyes nearly popped out of his head as he thought he'd come right there and then.

Lucas laughed.

"Do that again and it's all over," Christopher gasped, and meant it.

Lucas moved himself away then towards Christopher, setting the pace and depth, all the while Christopher kissed his neck and caressed his cock. They continued like this until Lucas said, "Faster. I want to feel you come inside me."

ALTHOUGH LUCAS WAS enjoying this, what he really wanted was to sit astride the hairy chest and bob up and down on his boyfriend's hard cock, enjoying the delicious pain of it stabbing into him with every movement. More than this, he wanted to feel his wonderful, caring, beautiful boyfriend coming inside of him. Coming because he'd made him come. Coming as he pumped himself into Lucas's body. And he knew that would never happen as they lay now on the bed.

He felt Christopher inside him retreat, soften, disconnect and turned to kiss him. He needed to feel that connection, that presence within himself. Where was Christopher going? He tightened those muscles and smiled as Christopher gasped, then soon reconnected with him, grew, hardened inside him. He changed his position, pushing Christopher onto his back so he could lower himself onto him. They separated and Lucas gasped with pleasure and anticipation at the full feeling he would soon have again.

Lowering himself onto Christopher, he crouched on either side of his hairy chest but noticed something in his eyes. Something that said he wasn't enjoying himself—a look of concentration you shouldn't have when making love. He continued to pleasure himself with Christopher's cock but noticed that it became more and more difficult as it softened until finally they separated.

Christopher turned away, not wanting to make eye contact. "Sorry."

Lucas shook his head, pulling Christopher to face him. "Nothing to be sorry about. Show me what you want and I will do it." Whatever it was that had gone wrong, Lucas was determined not to let it spoil what had up to that point been an amazing fuck. He had been so near, and so had Christopher, he felt sure, until...

Christopher lay on his side and positioned Lucas in front of him, his wet kisses and hot breath on his back. They rested skin to skin, no gap between Lucas's back and Christopher's chest for a few short moments until Lucas felt Christopher stiffen, deliciously rise to the occasion. Without any words, he lifted his legs up and pushed himself backwards onto the hot, stiff cock that had been giving him so much pleasure. Lucas nodded; if this was what Christopher liked, this would be how they'd do it—for now. He felt warm, safe, protected, loved, as Christopher wrapped his arms around Lucas's torso. He felt sexy, desired, powerful as Lucas pushed himself backwards to meet Christopher's forwards thrusts, and then pulled away as Christopher did the same. With each joining and separating, a wave of pleasure started from deep inside his abdomen, radiating out across his whole body until once again they repeated the movement and more pleasure waved through him.

They quickened their pace, now accompanied by Christopher pulling on Lucas's cock, forming a tunnel for him to thrust into while simultaneously thrusting backwards onto Christopher's cock. With no words exchanged, and one final deep thrust into Lucas, Christopher moaned and his legs shook as he came inside Lucas.

Lucas felt the pumping of his boyfriend's sperm leaving the cock, sending waves of warm pleasure radiating out from his prostate and in one final thrust for himself into Christopher's hands, he came so hard that he thought he'd faint.

They lay connected, Lucas enjoying the closeness, the oneness he felt with Christopher, for a while, and then gently they separated, kissed and fell asleep.

Finally, a man who can fuck me and make love to me at the same time, Lucas thought.

Christopher kissed him. "I love you."

"I love you too." *So why have I not told you about seeing Pedro in Madrid?*

The guilt that had disappeared during the sex—his body too occupied with pleasure then—returned and Lucas knew he must come clean with Christopher about Pedro. Soon.

Chapter Twelve

ALTHOUGH CHRISTOPHER WAS happy that Lucas had decided to stay on the island, he couldn't quite believe that he himself had been something Lucas had taken into account for the decision. "His mamá, I understand, but me?" Christopher shook his head, staring down at himself.

Sally squeezed his chin and shook her head. "When will you believe me when I tell you, you're worth staying for. You're a kind, generous, attractive man."

"I don't feel it. I'm just me."

"That's seven years with Dan making you feel inadequate. If someone tells you that you're useless for long enough, you'll soon start believing it. I rest my case."

"It's a lot to live up to, isn't it?"

Sally shrugged. "Love doesn't come with a guarantee, you know. You've just got to do your best, every day, be kind and humour each other, and take it a day at a time."

"Okay, I should write that down. Have you been reading *Eat, Pray. Love* or something?"

"After years of being with the wrong men it sort of came to me." Scrabbling for a pen to write it down she said, "I must remember it for future reference. Future boyfriends more like!" Slamming the pen down, she laughed.

"Now that you're single." Christopher thought for a moment about what Lucas had told him about why he wanted to stay. "I'm meant to be all spiritual, but really I sometimes wish I had my brand new BMW and my big apartment and enough money not to care about it. How spiritual is that?" He shrugged.

"It's a lapse. No one is perfect." Sally narrowed her eyes at him. "You're just trying to think of excuses for why it won't work. Then you can walk away easily."

Christopher shook his head. "I missed him so much when he was gone I almost forgot what it felt like to spoon him in bed at night." *And fucking him was pretty mind blowing too.* "He calms me. He gets me. He fits with me. We fit."

Sally sighed and ruffled his hair. "You're so cute. Alone and together. Fitting. It sounds so simple but is so hard to find."

LUCAS AND CHRISTOPHER were walking along the beach at Playa d'en Bossa, holding hands.

Lucas had been explaining it was the longest beach on the island and so very popular with tourists. They'd passed luxury hotels pools with Balinese beds covered in holidaymakers, then restaurants next to the sand and were now standing underneath one of the lifeguard stations—a tall wooden tower.

"I've never had someone change their plans for me," Christopher said.

"It wasn't only you. It was Mamá too," Lucas said. "You are my boyfriend, why wouldn't I want to come back to you?"

"I hope I live up to your expectations."

Lucas kissed him. "You already are." Staring out to sea for a moment, Lucas knew he had to come clean about seeing Pedro in Madrid. He looked out to sea.

"What's wrong?"

understand that. I'm sorry. I wanted to get it straight in my head first."

"If I'd have been there I'd have ended up in a fight. Probably both of us would have gone to jail. As long as you're okay."

Lucas nodded silently, then led him towards the quieter end of the beach.

WHILE LUCAS RAN into the sea, his tanned back facing him, Christopher replayed their conversation to himself. He felt both a burning desire to kiss Lucas all over as his back glistened wet in the sun, and a fiery hot anger at the thought of Pedro sticking his fingers in Lucas's mouth. He wished he could have been there to protect Lucas. If only he could have told the vile Pedro what to do. If only... Christopher stopped the thoughts and focussed on the now.

Lucas dived into the sea, disappeared completely then surfaced, waving his hands above his head and shouting for Christopher to join him.

Christopher texted Sally: *he saw the ex in Madrid. Assaulted him. Police etc.*

Sally replied: *OMG! Is he OK?*

Christopher replied: *yes. I'm so angry. I want to punch someone. The ex.*

Sally replied: *very mature. We'll talk.*

Christopher put his phone away, and was about to carefully remove his shorts and underwear underneath a towel to change into swimming shorts when he realised he hadn't brought any.

Damn.

His phone beeped again. A message from Sally: *at least he told you. People don't feel guilty about stuff they've done if they don't love the person it affects.*

"Nothing."

"Bollocks." Christopher took a deep breath. "After we've talked about, we can discuss anything."

Lucas agreed. The conversation about Christoph anxiety after the silver packet incident had been at fi awkward, but ultimately had resulted in a strong relationship and the closeness Lucas had needed from Christopher. Biting his lip, Lucas swallowed the lump in hi throat then said, "The guilt is killing me. I can't believe I let it happen. I never wanted to hurt you but... It's Pedro."

"Your ex. Words I'm not fond of hearing. Okay, what about him?"

"I saw him in Madrid. Well, he saw me." Lucas told him what had happened, ending with a quiet, "Someone called the police. I didn't want to make a fuss, but..."

"Were you hurt?"

"Not physically, no." Lucas shook his head.

Christopher tutted loudly, bunching his hands into fists. "But he assaulted you. From what you said, that's assault."

Lucas avoided eye contact.

"It wasn't your fault. No reason to feel guilty."

"I couldn't keep it from you. I had to..." Lucas said.

"He sounds vile." After a pause for reflection Christopher continued, "What did you ever see in him?"

"Honestly, now, I don't know." Lucas shrugged. "He' done much worse before. He kept push, push, pushing me. In a way it wasn't as bad as it could have been."

"How come?"

"He didn't have the power over me that he used to. used to tell me to do something and, well, I'd do it." Lu stared into Christopher's eyes, blinking away a tear should have told you before. It's still lying by omissi(

Christopher reread the text. Despite the pain and anger, Sally had a point. And that was the same reason he'd told Lucas about the nightclub incident.

And then it hit him: it would have been much simpler to just walk away each time. But instead, Lucas had chosen to stay with him after the night club incident, and Christopher, in turn, couldn't imagine a life without Lucas. He wasn't about to let something as stupid as Pedro get between him and Lucas. Not now, not ever.

He shrugged his T-shirt off, stepped out of his shorts and ran into the sea to join Lucas. "Second thoughts, I wanted to join you. The water looked so inviting."

"You didn't bring your swimming shorts?"

"I was going to go naked but had second, second thoughts."

Lucas laughed and swam close to him, hugged him towards himself, then kissed Christopher. "It is beautiful in here together."

Christopher nodded, holding on tightly to the man he loved more than he'd ever felt possible. "Thank you for telling me."

"I couldn't have kept it from you."

They splashed wordlessly for a few moments.

"Me neither."

THEY WERE IN a bar by the beach in San Antonio, watching the parades of Brits abroad walking past, drunk and sunburned.

"I need to see him." Christopher paused, reflecting on Lucas's news about Pedro assaulting him. Turning to Sally, he said, "I said the Pedro thing wasn't a big deal but really I..."

"Want to kill the piece-of-shit ex-boyfriend?" Sally raised her eyebrows.

"Hardly a spiritual approach. No, if I saw him I'd tell him to leave Lucas alone. Because..."

"He's yours?"

"He's not mine. People don't own other people. Because I want to protect Lucas. To love Lucas."

"Much more adult."

"Thing is, though, just the thought of Pedro touching him, hurting him, makes me want to punch him into next week. And I know that makes me as bad as him, but the anger is like this white hot ball in my stomach."

"Proves you care about him," Sally said. "Much better than not being bothered. That sort of passion is a good basis of a relationship. Count yourself lucky, I say."

"I don't ever remember feeling this protective or missing Dan this much. What does that say?" Christopher rolled his eyes.

"Tell him how much you love him. Explain how Pedro's abuse of him makes you feel. Not to smother him but to show him how you feel. Just because you're equals in the relationship doesn't mean there can't be a bit of protection."

"I don't want him to think I'm overpowering him like P...he used to."

"There's no danger of that, I'm sure." Sally finished her drink, pulled her bikini top up and said, "You coming for a swim?"

Nodding, he stood and said, "Yep. I think I need to calm down."

LATER THAT DAY, Christopher and Lucas sat on the rocks, looking out to the sun setting over the sea at Cala Conta.

Drums mixed with chill out music drifted up from the beach shack below by the sea. Small groups of people assembled along the rock edge facing the red sun above the deep blue sea.

"This is the best sunset on Ibiza. It was used in the Wham! video for "Club Tropicana"." Lucas hummed the chorus about the drinks being free.

Christopher nodded in recognition.

"It is better here in winter when the tourists leave. They give the island back to the locals. To me." Lucas smiled.

"To us." Christopher squeezed Lucas's hand.

"Winter will be quiet for us." Lucas held Christopher's hand. "There is very little dancing work then. Most of the clubs close. I haven't heard from Sasha about her plans. Probably, these will come to nothing."

"It doesn't matter." Christopher pressed his fingers on Lucas's.

"We must eat. We must pay rent."

"I can write for English clients. And *Ibiza Discovered* will need people to work during winter. We are down to three of us now at the office."

"I will work in the bar. If it closes I will clean villas and hotels. There will be a light installation in Ibiza Town during winter—maybe I can perform with that?"

"We will work. We'll be together. It will be fine."

"Did I tell you how I danced in Madrid when I visited Mamà?"

"No."

"I hated it. It reminded me why I left. I couldn't have stayed even if I had to. I was always coming back here—the island called me."

"Me too. When I left the UK, I stuck a pin in the map and it landed on Ibiza. First time."

As the sun set in a mix of reds, oranges, and purples above the sea, the crowds clapped and a few people cheered.

"Throw your heart out in front of yourself and run after it." His mamá's words from her bedside echoed through his mind.

He'd thrown it far in front of himself and here, on the edge of the island, with the sun disappearing into the sea, was where he found himself now; right next to Christopher, the man who was loving him more and more every single day.

Chapter Thirteen

A FEW DAYS later, Christopher walked into the covered market and was hit with the smells of a mixture of sandalwood, marijuana, and spices. The hippy market was in full swing and he was here to write about it for *Ibiza Discovered*. There were rows of stalls selling handmade pottery, hand woven rugs and clothes and a section against the far wall selling food. The smell of gently cooking paella made Christopher hungry.

He slowly walked past the stands, picking up their wares, asking the stall holders about them before moving onto the next stand. His boss at *Ibiza Discovered* had told him they needed more non-clubbing related articles to try to make the island a year-round destination rather than only for the summer clubbing season.

"Once all the closing parties are done, what will you do?" his boss had asked Christopher.

Christopher had shrugged. "I don't want to go back to London. To that city. To that work. To that life." He didn't want to say any more about the ex because sometimes even now it still upset him thinking about it.

"You don't have to go back to the UK—could you move to Madrid with Lucas?" his boss said.

Christopher knew that wasn't really an option for Lucas because of the ex and because Ibiza had been his dream life. And because if he met Pedro, he wasn't sure he could keep control of his temper. "Will there be work here?"

"Less than in summer. But we need articles all year round."

Now, as Christopher put down a pink tie-dyed T-shirt, Lucas rang.

"Sascha's offered me something for November and December. I don't know about January and February yet. No one seems to know about January and February yet. I think the island goes into low power mode or something. We could go back to the UK then and save money." It all tumbled out of his mouth together in a breathless mass.

"Have you spent a January and February in the UK?"

"No. Why?"

"They're the worst months for weather—snow, sleet, rain, ice, dark by four o'clock." *Plus I'd find myself calling up old friends from the City, and being offered something temporary in one of the banks and before I knew it I'd be back in a grey suit, commuting to Liverpool Street as my soul slowly seeped from my body.*

"Oh. But...what will we do?" Lucas asked.

"We'll stay here and..." Christopher looked up and caught the eye of a woman selling Greixonera—a traditional Ibizan dessert of Spanish cinnamon Danish pastries soaked and baked in milk, eggs and sugar that he enjoyed most days—and he knew he wasn't about to leave all this for a cold dark UK winter. "We will think of something." Christopher closed his eyes for a moment and concentrated on the universe swirling around him. He knew something would come up to allow them to stay on the island for winter. It had to. "We won't return to Madrid. I know how you don't want that." *Neither do I.*

"It's best for me not to return there," Lucas said.

"Look, gotta go, I've yet to get halfway around this market." He ended the call. Christopher made his way around the market, impressed by the variety of goods on offer including some beaded jewellery, throws and mini fishing nets with coloured beads that hung from the ceiling. He turned one of these contraptions between his hands. "What is it?"

The stall holder—a woman in her thirties with dreadlocked brown hair, pierced lip and a long red dress— said, "It's a dream catcher. Haven't you seen them before in the UK?"

In the world he'd left in the UK, a dream catcher was a bank account full of money, a perfect deal grabbed on the trading room floor, a brochure for a new Mercedes, not some feathers and a bit of fishing net. "No."

"Haven't seen you here before. New on the island, are you?"

"A year or so. I didn't know this was here until my boss told me to come and cover it. Shame it's too late to get publicity for people to come." He looked around the market at most stalls with people gathering in front of them. "Pretty busy, though."

The woman rolled her eyes. "Wait until winter. It's dead. January and February there's so little to do outside, even though it's still sunny. Cos we still get three hundred days of sunshine a year, even in winter!"

Christopher winked, in recognition at one of Ibiza's most-quoted facts.

She handed him the dream catcher. "Take it. Make sure you write about my amazing stall and all the great stuff I'm selling."

"I will, thanks." He offered to pay her.

She waved his money away with a smile. "I say there's nothing to do in winter, but," she was whispering now, "it's my favourite part of the year."

"Why?" Christopher frowned, ready to write a note on his paper pad.

"No bloody tourists. The island is ours again. It's so peaceful, quiet, restful."

"Does nobody come here for winter?"

"Walkers, people wanting to escape from it all. But mainly it's about the Ibizan residents getting their island back until the start of a new season of clubbing and sunning and touristing."

Christopher made a few notes on the paper, thanked the woman and moved towards the next stand, selling jars of Ibizan honey. As he tasted the fudge-like sweetness on a tiny plastic fork, his mind ticked over about what to do during the island's quietest and most magical time of the year.

He knew he would have to get past the anger he felt for Pedro. A man he'd not even met but had managed to invoke in him a white hot rage like nothing he'd felt before. Christopher had never felt such rage because he realised now he'd never loved anyone like he loved Lucas. And he'd never loved anyone as much because he hadn't fitted so well with someone who he felt able to open up to emotionally.

All of this led him to the conclusion that he mustn't let the anger he felt for Pedro's actions boil over and spoil his relationship with Lucas.

LUCAS ENDED THE call, stubbed his cigarette out on the ground and walked back into the bar. "Do you stay open over winter?"

The manager nodded and continued drying glasses with a tea towel.

"Will you need me then?" Even though it wasn't what he'd dreamed of doing, the bar work could allow he and

Christopher to stay in Ibiza all year round. And that was the most important thing.

"We're open Friday, Saturday, and Sunday in winter. The locals need places to eat out, but there's not many other customers."

"I want to be a local for winter. Can I work here too?" Lucas held his breath for a moment.

"We'll see. I don't know if I will stay, or go to the Canary Islands for winter and close up completely. I'll let you know." He turned to serve a customer at the far end of the bar.

The rest of Lucas's shift passed unremarkably; he served customers drinks, took their food orders and did his best to become absolutely indispensable to the manager by offering to do a whole host of little extra jobs during quiet periods. The manager side-eyed Lucas as he too enthusiastically cleaned the dishwasher filters before volunteering to clean the inside of the two large meat fridges at the back of the kitchen.

On his way home he called his sister Maria. "I can't believe it. My dream is over. I might as well have stayed in Madrid when I visited Mamá. I will have to return for winter. Christopher, he says we will be fine, work will come, but I don't believe this."

"Slow down. Calm down. What's happened?"

He told her about the lack of work in winter and what his boss had said about the bar.

After listening in silence, Maria held her breath and then said, "Dear brother, although it might feel like it, the world is not ending. Always with the dramatics! Besides, I'm visiting you in January. I've already booked my flight."

"You didn't tell me!" Lucas threw his hands in the air. "Why not! I'd have told you not to come. You can't visit me then, there's nothing to do. Ibiza is about summer and sunshine and dancing and clubbing. None of that happens in winter. For fuck's sake, Maria."

"I will be spending time with my brother, away from Mamá and Papá, a holiday alone. I don't care what we do as long as it's just us."

Lucas sighed at an argument he knew he'd not win; such was her tenacity. "I've got to work because I don't want to owe Christopher more than I already owe him." Lucas knew how important it was to both he and Christopher to have a relationship of equals and despite Christopher saying they would manage on his own money during winter, Lucas wanted to contribute his fair share.

"Why did he lend you money, again?"

"Flights to see Mamá."

"How about I lend you some to pay back Christopher, so you owe me instead. Better?" She smiled at a plan well executed and uncrossed her fingers, slowly starting to dance around the room.

"Better." Even though Christopher had never mentioned the money, Lucas knew he still owed it. And repaying him felt like the best sort of thanks, despite Christopher's pleas that he didn't need repaying and that Lucas did more than enough to repay him already. "He said that he doesn't need me to repay him but..."

"Very kind of him. But?"

"But," Lucas said, biting his lip, "Pedro had all this power over me. I know Christopher isn't Pedro, but I want us to be in a level relationship. I know he wouldn't behave like Pedro did, but if we're making a life together I want us to make a life together. Make sense?"

"It does. How are you making a life together?" Maria asked.

"I don't want to leave. I want to be here, for the whole year. I don't want to live here like a tourist, I want to really live here. And if I have to leave in winter, that's not like a local, is it?"

"I suppose not. Worst case scenario—" Maria said.

"Words I'm never fond of hearing..." Lucas shook his head and held his breath.

"Worst case, would Christopher come back to Madrid with you?"

"Probably. I would if it was the other way round. If we needed to go to the UK because Christopher couldn't stay, I'd be on a flight to London straight away."

"That's not what I asked," Maria said.

"He came here to get out of the city, the rat race, and he's enjoying the spirituality of Ibiza. I don't know if he'd get that in Madrid."

"We have sunsets here too." Maria laughed.

"Over the sea? With beaches? And with a purple, red and orange sky?" Lucas shook his head. *And Pedro.*

"You know we don't."

'I'm here now. We'll talk again about your visit."

"It'll come round soon." Maria ended the call.

Lucas arrived at the apartment Christopher shared with Sally and wondered how all these unknowns in his life would become solid knowns, or whether they'd carry on swirling around in the morass of change he was now experiencing.

And among all the uncertainty, he knew the one thing that was certain was Christopher and his love. He just hoped that, and some sort of a plan, could allow them to stay over winter.

A FEW DAYS later, Lucas and Christopher were cuddled up together on the sofa at Christopher's place, discussing the arrival of Maria and whether she could sleep there, or squeeze into Lucas's place. Lucas didn't want to put Christopher out with his sister staying, but equally wasn't sure if sharing a bed in a studio apartment with his sister would make for an enjoyable holiday.

Christopher said, "She can sleep here in my room and I'll move in with you," simply, before realising how big that really sounded.

They sat in silence holding hands on the sofa, considering this for a moment when Sally bustled in, singing the chorus of "Wannabe" by the Spice Girls and carrying bags of shopping.

"I see the love birds are nesting comfortably!"

Christopher extricated himself from Lucas's arms and they both sat upright on the sofa. "Good day?"

"Don't mind me. I'm happy for you. For both of you." She put the shopping bags on the kitchen table and began unpacking them. "What were you talking about Maria staying here?"

"My sister," Lucas said, and then explained about her flying over to visit in January.

"We thought she might stay here," Christopher said. "But I was going to check with you first, of course."

"Don't worry about that. I won't be here."

"Where are you going?"

"None of us will be here. It's in the tenancy agreement we both signed." Sally stared at Christopher. "Remember?"

Christopher racked his brain for anything about the tenancy agreement and retrieved nothing. He remembered the rent being very reasonable for that part of Ibiza town and had been impressed at the view of the port from the balcony, but that was all.

"This whole area, this whole block is closing for winter. It's all holiday rentals. They're refurbishing it over winter in preparation for next year's tourists. Everyone's out in two weeks." Sally stood with her hand on her hip. "There are signs on the lifts. I'm going back to the UK. Didn't you notice me packing? I did tell you."

Christopher shook his head. Last winter the apartment he'd rented hadn't done this, so why was the too-good-to-be-true current apartment? He'd noticed boxes appearing in the hallway but had thought nothing of it as he'd been so busy trying to work out a plan to stay during the low season. And spending time at Lucas's place. In his bed. Some days when they could they would spend a lazy afternoon in bed together, only leaving the room for food and drink. He'd not even thought about accommodation. He'd assumed that would all be fine. No reason to think otherwise.

Sally sat at the kitchen table and took a bite of an apple. After chewing thoughtfully, she said, "You've been in your own little world for a while." She stared at Lucas. "A nice little world. A world of the two love birds."

"I will go." Lucas stood.

"It's nothing to do with you." Sally motioned for him to sit down. "Really it's not personal—this block closes and everyone's gotta leave. It is what it is." She shrugged. "It's been lovely getting to know you properly." She nodded at Christopher, who ducked his head in embarrassment. "But it's nice to witness it first hand; to really see how happy you make him."

Lucas turned to Christopher with a smile. "There was me thinking he was playing it cool."

"Oh no, I've heard all about you. Every date, every kiss, every…" She licked the apple seductively before biting a bit off and keeping eye contact with Lucas. "Days spent in

Christopher's room, or disappeared together at your place, Lucas. I knew you'd both eventually surface for food. You've both been pretty...preoccupied." She laughed, a high pitched trill. "You two loll around on the sofa all you like." Sally kissed Lucas on the cheek on her way to her bedroom while singing another Spice Girls song.

WITH SO LITTLE time to organise anything else, Christopher moved into Lucas's studio flat. They agreed it was the logical next step for them and that they'd been spending so much time together anyway, "My bed, your bed, my wardrobe your wardrobe? What difference does it make? Of course you can move in with me," Lucas had said.

Sally left with a promise to return next summer ("I'll call when I land at the airport, you can pick me up, I'm not letting you get away from me that easily my loves!") leaving boxes of things she couldn't take back.

Now, these boxes stood in Lucas's studio room next to Christopher's boxes, or stacked on top of the few pieces of furniture Christopher had taken from the flat.

Lucas lazily pulled a comb through his hair in front of the mirror. The lack of floor space in the studio room apparent by him stepping backwards and falling over two boxes and onto the bed where Christopher sat cross legged, writing an article on his laptop.

"Sorry," Christopher said. "I'll move my things when you're at work."

Lucas kissed him on the lips. "Your things, my things; it's our apartment." He said goodbye and left for his shift at the bar.

The door banging woke Christopher from his concentration, staring at the screen, mid-article about the walking trails around Ibiza for out of season travellers. He'd really put a lot of work into it to make it interesting, especially since he wasn't much of a walker himself, so he'd spoken to some locals who knew the best trails to put together the piece. As he wrote the last sentence and added a full stop, he felt a sense of satisfaction he'd never felt at his investment banker job in London. Interviewing locals and sampling restaurants and clubs was so much more interesting than poring over reports and spreadsheets about numbers and exchange rates.

He climbed off the bed and tripped on the boxes Lucas had tumbled over earlier. *I really must work out what's in them soon.* As he made himself a café cortado condensada—an espresso with condensed milk which had become a regular sweet guilty pleasure that Lucas had introduced him to—he thought about the next article he needed to write.

Absentmindedly he swept his gaze around the room: hardly any floor space, clothes strewn over the bed and sofa from earlier impromptu sex and he decided to tidy up before writing the restaurant review of where he and Lucas had eaten last night.

As he folded clothes, emptied the contents of boxes into their right places and listened to the radio, he felt a warmth radiating through his chest. A deep satisfaction at what he was doing at that moment, in that place.

He made himself a chorizo paprika sausage and manchego sheep's milk cheese sandwich which he ate, perched on the kitchen worktop, staring out at the green hills peppered with small villages. The sweet paprika sausage contrasted perfectly with the creamy texture and distinctive sheep flavour of the cheese.

Everything he owned, everything that mattered to him—except Lucas, who was at work—was in this apartment. No matter how hard he'd worked, how many designer clothes he'd bought, how many new cars he'd driven off the forecourt, he'd never felt as happy as he did now at this moment.

As he cleaned up the kitchen he read a note from Lucas: *my letter and CV please! xLx*

Sipping the sweet coffee, he settled at the now clear table in the corner and started to write Lucas an application letter and CV in English for the summer season at Amnesia and Pacha. He smiled as he wrote up Lucas's experience from his rough Spanish notes beside him on the table. "Why can't I just dance for the interview?" Lucas had said, as he told Christopher his experience for the "stupid, pointless application letters".

"I will do it, you dance and tell me what you did," Christopher had replied, frantically writing in Spanish as Lucas babbled away.

"They want me to write letters in the club? What is this bullshit?" Lucas had said.

Christopher had waved it away and said he'd have them done by the time Lucas returned from work. Now, when he looked at the clock, he realised it was only four hours away.

Bullshit, the same as Lucas worrying about paying him back for the flights. But Lucas had insisted and handed him the cash, explaining that he had to repay him and no a month of blowjobs wasn't considered payback. "I must pay you back for me, even if you do not need it," Lucas had said with a smile.

And Christopher had nodded, understanding completely why it was important to him they be equals in their relationship; accepting the money in silence.

Chapter Fourteen

AS IBIZA CHANGED down a gear for autumn, they started to attend a supper club in a restaurant behind the church in San Jose, which was a small inland village nestled high in the hills, a short drive from Lucas's apartment. The supper club was for British and Spanish residents of Ibiza who had all complained about the lack of reasons to meet up in the daytime during winter without spending lots of money. The restaurant put on a tasting menu for customers to sample small bits of their whole menu.

"I want somewhere to just be, without always having to sit around eating and drinking wine," a man said at the supper club.

"I don't want to have one glass of cool wine in winter and drive home in the dark. I've spent the whole day sitting at home waiting to come out in the evening when there's nothing to do during the day," a woman added while refusing the rest of her wine on grounds of driving later.

"They all said they'd speak Spanish," Lucas added, putting his hand on Christopher's arm. "But they talked in English for the whole night. I sat with a Spanish girlfriend spitting on the ignorant English people."

"You loved her. Your English is better than my Spanish," Christopher said. Christopher had been meaning to really get into spirituality since before he arrived in Ibiza. He'd bought a few books, and he'd even put them by his bedside table. Unfortunately, he'd never got round to reading much of them. He was always so busy working, partying, arguing with Dan, to ever think about sitting down and reading a book about mindfulness or meditation, or yoga, or pilates, or any of the other things his ex used to so attractively call, "A load of bollocks and a total waste of time."

However, since being in Ibiza, Christopher had rekindled his interest in spirituality and had been making time to read. One in particular had really sunken into his consciousness and made its way into his every day life: *Mindfulness Matters,* by someone with a Greek sounding name, had made it to Christopher's bedside cabinet. Even after he'd finished it, he kept referring to its teachings and reminding his mind to return to the now, the here, and simply that.

On their way back from their third or fourth visit to the supper club at the start of autumn, Christopher asked Lucas if he thought an idea he'd had was mad.

"Tell me, and then I'll tell you." Lucas stroked Christopher's cheek.

"Three hundred and twenty, or three hundred days of sunshine a year and during winter we're all sat inside waiting to go out in the evenings to these social things. The tastings at restaurants, the supper clubs, they're all during the evenings. What about if we do something for Ibiza residents in winter, during the day?"

"A market? I'm not running a market stall with you. Or a shop. My friend tried that in Madrid, up at five, back at three, lugging boxes everywhere and all for less than she'd have made serving coffees. No thank you."

"Like a retreat, for people who live here." Christopher struggled to find the name for what he meant.

"A retreat without the retreat." Lucas sighed dramatically. "We are so going to the UK this winter."

"A retreat with the bits people want, but without the staying overnight stuff. Same as how you don't want to run a market stall, I'm not interested in running a hotel. But the meditation and mindfulness stuff, I reckon I could do that. Bit of socialising too, some food, and you could do some yoga or movement and dance classes."

"I could." Lucas perked up. "Clever boy." Lucas kissed him.

Blushing, Christopher pulled back from the kiss and replied, "I couldn't do it without you, though."

And so, after some looking they found an old church hall next to a church in San Rafael, an unfashionable village a while from the coast where tourists only ventured for a renowned restaurant. The community was over the moon to have their village as a destination during winter.

"It's also twenty minutes from most main towns; it's like some sort of equidistant Ibiza triangle or something." Christopher shrugged after studying the location on a map.

"We have found our location!" Lucas stamped his feet on the ground and did a little flamenco dance in celebration as Christopher's heart melted.

ON THE FIRST Monday in November, long after the night clubs had held their closing parties, the tourists had left and the island returned to its alternative, hippy, laidback Balearic vibe, Mindfulness Movement & Munching was born. Or, *Atención Plena Movimiento Comiendo*, for the Spanish who attended.

The white hall behind the church had easily held the first fifteen people who came to that class.

They started with Christopher giving an introduction to mindfulness. "It is about trying to remain conscious of the present moment, keeping your mind from thinking about the past or the future, simply staying in the now." He went on to explain the difference between formal and informal practice: "Formal is when you choose to spend time meditating, or just sitting if you want to call it, but sitting and only thinking about the now. Noticing the breaths you take in and out, feeling the cool against your skin, or a breeze on your face. Informal is about using the teachings to be mindful in our everyday lives—when you're at work, when you're walking the dog, when you're having a meal with friends."

Lucas puffed out his chest with pride, then bowed at the back of the hall next to a table covered in tapas he'd prepared. "There is food afterwards. We will be watching you to check how mindful you are. Joking!"

After almost an hour of mindfulness exercises and teachings, Christopher handed over control to Lucas who took the class through movements, stretches, breathing and some simple choreographed moves he'd used in dance routines. "This is to work up your appetites," he said. "Or you would all fall asleep." And the class copied Lucas's movements to music and occasional laughter.

To make sure the class was inclusive of both British residents and Spanish native Ibizans, the instructions were in both Spanish and English. At first the classes mainly consisted of British people, but as word spread about the two men's classes and tapas lunches, more and more Spanish people joined.

A few weeks after starting, the hall was soon full and they had to introduce a booking system and then added classes on Wednesdays and Fridays, so by the end of the winter, they were holding classes of fifty, three times a week, all in a hall in little old unfashionable San Raphael.

One afternoon, over tapas, somebody asked Christopher what had interested him in Mindfulness.

He took a breath, closed his eyes, then replied, "I spent my whole life rushing from one activity to the next. When I was at work I was rushing to get off the phone and onto the next thing. When I was at home I was rushing people out the door to get back to my laptop. And when I left it all, I realised I didn't know what I was actually rushing towards." *And only now do I know what real true love feels like with Lucas.*

"Did it feel like you were always running to catch a flight or something?"

"Exactly that! But I'd never stopped long enough to think about it, or why, or where I was running from and to. That's the thing about ceaseless activity it doesn't end and we think we've got to carry on doing it, but don't know why. When I got to Ibiza, I suddenly had whole days full of nothing. It was terrifying at first, but I got used to it eventually."

"How do you do it? I found myself worrying about whether I was doing it right, when you were saying to only think about standing in the hall, and I really wanted to just think about standing there, but then I was worried about other things."

Christopher smiled. This was something he'd experienced at the start. "That itself is something you can recognise and bring your mind back to the now. The mind is hard wired to think. The worries and anxieties are what makes us feel bad. But they are only thoughts. They aren't real."

Lucas appeared at his side, carrying Trevor, their black and white Papillon dog. "I think it can all be summed up by—live like a dog. Dogs don't worry about the future, or go over the past. They live in the now, enjoy every moment." The dog barked and Lucas turned to him and stroked his head. "That's right, Trevor." Lucas shook his head.

The woman thanked them both and returned to the far end of the hall where others were sitting in groups, eating, drinking and chatting. She picked up her knitting and joined a few others who were doing the same in the corner. Another group were threading beads and stones onto leather to create necklaces and bracelets.

Lucas looked up to Christopher. "We did it. We really did! We built this together. Side by side."

"I told you something would work out." Christopher kissed him, with a glint in his eye that meant only one thing. "I knew that together we'd do it."

"I fucking love you." Lucas flashed the naughty smile he always did at moments like this.

"And I love fucking you." Christopher pulled him closer, pressing his straining cock against Lucas's arse once he'd manoeuvred himself into their favourite standing pose: Christopher's arms wrapped around Lucas's chest.

They made their way back to the apartment where they were soon naked, standing facing the edge of the room, Lucas's hands resting on the wall as Christopher stood behind him as he thrust deep into Lucas, kissing his neck. Christopher loved hearing how much pleasure this gave Lucas, all anxiety gone, as he enjoyed how they fitted together physically as well as emotionally.

Chapter Fifteen

MARIA ARRIVED IN January as promised, which was the quietest month for tourism on the island, along with February. At the airport, she greeted Lucas and Christopher, hugging them in turn. "I didn't think it would be sunny still!" She looked at their sunglasses, perched on their heads.

"Three hundred days of sunshine a year," Christopher said with a smile.

On the journey back, Maria stared out of the window. "The plane was half empty. I kept thinking they'd announce it was cancelled and I'd have to catch a boat or something." She laughed.

Lucas turned to face his sister in the back seat. "I told you there's not much happening at this time of the year. I hope you're not bored."

"When did you last see me at a night club?"

"But that's why everyone comes here, isn't it?"

Christopher pointed to the empty beach they were passing. "That, in summer, you couldn't see the sand. It was covered in beach towels and people. Now, the island is ours." He looked at Maria in the rear view mirror. "Yours too." He smiled.

"I came here for a rest. I came to get away from the busyness of Madrid, of the city dirt, of all the bloody people I am sick and tired of bumping into. Sometimes I feel like I can't breathe living there."

Lucas shrugged. "Plenty of room to breathe here in winter."

MARIA DUMPED HER bag on the floor of their apartment. "I don't know how you've managed it, but it feels full yet you don't have any furniture except"—she turned a full circle around the room—"bed, sofa, chairs, table." After a pause, she added, "And lots of boxes. What's with all these boxes?"

Lucas explained about Sally leaving her things and Christopher moving in with his. "Both apartments were unfurnished, and we've not got round to...furnishing this one yet. We don't know how long we'll be here." He looked at the ground. "At one point, we didn't even think we'd be here now."

Maria walked to her brother, squeezed his cheek. "You must always treat everywhere you live, even if it's for a night, like your own. Otherwise you never feel settled. When I went backpacking around Europe, someone I met told me that. It means you don't feel temporary everywhere."

"What about if we have to move?" Lucas asked.

"You do the same there. You paint the walls." Maria clapped. "You buy the curtains. This is your home. Treat it like one." She clapped again. "Understand?"

Christopher, who'd been in the kitchen preparing some chorizo stew and roast potatoes with a spicy tomato sauce, looked up from the pan. "Do you want to visit the markets and car boot sales with us?"

"She wants to relax." Lucas slumped on the sofa and lit a cigarette, thinking about his life, the apartment, how contented he was. He looked at Christopher busy in the kitchen and his heart almost burst with pride. *He's making Mama's patatas bravas!*

Maria folded her arms across her chest. "*She*, can speak for herself, thank you very much. And *she* would love to. Just the sort of thing *she*'d never have time for back home."

THE NEXT DAY they drove to a market selling home-made artisan goods: cheeses, honey, carved wooden bowls, glass ornaments of bulls and sunsets as well as some dried cured meats.

Maria bought a selection of food for their lunch and picked up and inspected everything on most stalls but didn't buy anything else. ("Hand luggage allowance only," and "I can't afford that," or "Beautiful but I'd break it in an instant.")

"That was a bit pointless if we didn't buy anything," Lucas said laying on a blanket under the shade of a tree while chewing a garlic-stuffed olive.

Christopher laughed and packed away his notebook he'd been writing on in case he wanted to write up the market for *Ibiza Discovered*.

Maria shook her head. "I still enjoyed it. I bought the food. I'm not really into buying more things. I've got a room full of things back home. I want to move myself to being more experiential with life." After a pause, she added, "Or try to anyway." She smirked and laughed.

"Same with us." Lucas lit a cigarette.

Christopher frowned. "It's very now, very millennial generation." He winked at Maria who winked back.

As she cut the bread for Christopher to have more, Maria said, "Experiences. Like this, are worth so much more than another necklace to add to the thirty-four I already own. Or another dress to the seventy-six I have hanging in my wardrobe."

Lucas nodded. "Ready for another experience?"

She nodded.

"Tomorrow, an Ibizan car boot sale." He stood, stamping his feet on the ground and performing a brief flamenco dance for them.

They clapped in appreciation.

"Don't ever change," Christopher said with a smile. "I love that your personality is bigger than your body." *Your beautiful, small, smooth body.*

"I couldn't change even if I tried." Lucas sat next to Christopher and kissed him.

THE CARS WERE parked with their rears facing each other around the edge of a red earth clearing in San Antonio. The town—which was renowned for its Brits abroad, partying and misbehaving—took on a somewhat different vibe during winter.

Lucas was reluctant to join Maria and Christopher. He couldn't see how they'd find anything interesting among the rubbish and unwanted things of others. "Why don't we buy it all from Ikea?"

"Because," Maria replied, "dear brother, thank God there isn't one on the island and it's about as soulless as you can get. Wouldn't you rather fill your home with things that have a story behind them? Things that have a soul, a history, some character?"

"I suppose." And so, because it pleased his sister and Christopher seemed enthusiastic too, having run off with her hand in hand, Lucas followed them to the car boot sale.

Maria's eye for a bargain and beauty picked out a white oval-shaped wardrobe with mirrored doors and mother of pearl handles that, Lucas had to admit, now he was looking at it, would be better than the clothes rail they had currently.

She also chose a black leather office chair that looked quite battered, but which still adjusted in all the ways it should. "It has supported a lot of people writing a lot of things. Christopher, you must have it for your office."

The office she referred to was, strictly speaking, a corner of the main studio room in which Christopher perched on a stool underneath a wooden trestle table that squeaked and moved every time he typed. Christopher had told her it was fine, but it definitely didn't meet Maria's make-yourself-at-home-straight-away philosophy, so the chair was purchased too, along with a matching roll top writing desk in which Christopher eventually put his laptop and stationery, cleanly hidden when not in use.

As they walked back to the car, Christopher realised the three of them and the three pieces of furniture would definitely not fit in their little Seat Ibiza. He offered to drive the furniture back while Maria and Lucas had a coffee and waited.

"I'll go, you two can catch up without me. As long as you help me load the car." Christopher smiled as Lucas kissed him on the cheek.

"Sometimes I love you even more than I thought possible," Lucas said.

WITH CHRISTOPHER LOADED up and departed, Maria disappeared to get coffees and returned holding a wooden box. It was about the same size as a laptop, but a hand-span deep. It had a diamond pattern of dark wood cross lines, light wood inside the diamonds, and each time a line crossed the intersection it was filled with mother of pearl. Maria placed it carefully on the table. "It's for both of you."

Lucas kissed her cheek. "You didn't need to."

"I know. That's why I did it. I thought you could put keys in it because you're both always losing your car and apartment keys. Maybe pens too because there's never one where you need it in your place."

Lucas took a sip of his coffee, walked to the counter and returned shortly afterwards with a pen and piece of till receipt the cashier had given him. On the paper he wrote for a while, slowly and deliberately, taking his time to get the words right and make sure it was legible for others. Finally he put it in the box and closed the lid.

"Don't I get to read it?" Maria asked.

"If you want. But I think my idea is better than your keys and pens idea." Lucas smiled as Maria opened the box and read out the note.

Wiping a tear from her cheek, Maria put the paper back in the box and closed the lid. "Much better idea."

Lucas had written the three biggest hopes and dreams he'd had since coming to Ibiza: To find love as well as sex with one man. To find someone who will let me dream and dance. To experience life as it is meant to be.

"What now?" Maria asked. "Do we light a candle? Burn some incense? Say a prayer?"

"If you want, but I'm just going to put it in the box and when I'm having a hard time and when I want to give it all up and come back to Mamá and Papá's, I'll open the box and remind myself why I'm here. And why I'm staying."

Maria nodded. "Will you ask Christopher to do the same?"

"I could write his for him now, he told me."

Maria handed her brother the pen and paper and Lucas wrote Christopher's hopes and dreams since moving to

Ibiza: To live a simple life. To find a man who is my equal partner in life. To live for love not for possessions.

Lucas put the paper in the box and closed the lid.

AFTER A FEW days of doing very little, they went to Santa Eulalia for lunch, which Christopher explained was the richest borough in the whole of Spain.

Maria, over fresh scallops in a restaurant on the smart promenade, said, "But will they have pretty dresses?"

Lucas scooped a scallop from its shell and plopped it into his mouth. "I thought you were all about experiences, not things." He gave his sister the side-eye.

"Yeah, but another pretty dress would fit so easily in my suitcase. Can we look afterwards?"

They ate Christopher's favourite dessert—greixonera. He had become quite the connoisseur of them, sampling them in every restaurant that served it. He finished his last mouthful. "Basically it's like bread and butter pudding. Do you have that in mainland Spain?"

Lucas and Maria shook their heads.

Maria chased her last spoonful around the plate, then ate it. "Is it as good as this?"

Christopher explained bread and butter pudding to them. They listened in silence until Lucas said, "Sounds like yesterday's sandwiches covered in milk. No thanks!"

Christopher promised to make it for them later during that week while Maria was staying with them.

Full of food, they left for the shops where Maria bought a very small, very white, very expensive slip dress by Calvin Klein. It made her look so beautiful that a man in the shop who'd been waiting for his wife in the changing room turned to Christopher and said, "You are a lucky man. If not for you, I would like to have her as my wife."

Before Christopher could explain he was gay and she was his boyfriend's sister, the man had disappeared, leaving all three of them laughing while Maria handed over her credit card.

As they returned to the apartment, Lucas turned to his sister. "You would have hated that place during summer."

"Why?" Maria removed the dress from the string-handled, paper bag and sniffed it. "Something about the smell of new clothes I love!"

"Busier than Madrid. Full of tourists. You'd have waited for hours for a changing room. Queues out the door sometimes. And sales—forget it. You'd have paid full price, no matter how much you'd wanted it."

Maria had been pleased at the 50 percent discount she'd got on the dress.

Christopher smiled to himself as Maria and Lucas chatted about the day. Ibiza in winter was turning out to be a pleasure all of its own, just as he'd hoped.

AT THE END of February, before Maria flew back to Madrid, they drove to the Valley of Santa Ines to view the almond blossom. As they turned a corner, Maria caught her breath. In front of them, as far as they could see were rows and rows of trees covered in white flowers.

Maria gasped. "It's like clouds!"

They parked by the side of the road. Maria jumped out and began taking pictures with her phone.

Christopher watched her as she spun from one direction to the next, clicking away on her camera all the while. "Spring is on its way."

Lucas stood next to Christopher, leaning against his chest and snuggled under his arm. "We made it through the winter, didn't we?"

"Told you we would." Christopher leant down and kissed Lucas, closing his eyes and inhaling the cool breeze and enjoying the sun's warmth on his skin. Spring was definitely on its way, and winter had been its own special kind of magic on Ibiza, as so many of the locals had told them.

After a while, Maria returned to the car. "The love birds are back, I see."

"Sorry, we've been sharing our bedroom with you for a few weeks, so..." Lucas trailed off, realising there was no good way to end that sentence.

"You only had to say. I'll give you some space when we get back. Leave me on a beach. I can write, or call Mamá, or read...." She waved absentmindedly into the distance. "Anyway, you said you had something to tell me about that had been your savour through winter here. And then you didn't tell me."

Christopher laughed. "I remember. We forgot, because we've been so busy doing nothing with you. It's exhausting all this relaxing and nothing we've done together."

"What will you do during summer?" Maria asked. "What about your dancing?"

Lucas shrugged and exhaled slowly. "Who knows? I'm sure it'll all work out in the end. Summer is a few months away and we're still enjoying the island as it sleeps and is ours."

"I think I won't visit you during summer because it's so beautiful now I wouldn't want to spoil that memory. I want this—you two, the almond blossoms, the classes you set up, the community you've joined—to be my memory of Ibiza."

Christopher told her she was welcome any time and they got back into the car and drove through the white clouds of almond blossom back to their apartment.

ON MARIA'S FINAL day, they dropped her at Ibiza airport and, holding hands, waved her into the departures area.

Christopher squeezed Lucas's hand. "Finally, we have the apartment all to ourselves." He raised his eyebrows.

Lucas laughed. "We must make use of it."

That afternoon, they made love to each other with their whole bodies, slowly and sensually. Lucas crouched over Christopher's chest plunging himself up and down on his lover's cock. Christopher's worries about his performance long since gone and Lucas relieved to have a man who was in his heart, his bed, and his head.

Chapter Sixteen

THE WINTER PASSED and their classes continued during spring, growing into more of a day time community event two or three times a week after the classes Christopher and Lucas took. They met other residents from all over Ibiza and soon found themselves invited to friends' homes throughout the island. Sometimes they complained they were too busy and that it was meant to be the low season, but once Christopher said, "It's hardly dancing all night with twenty thousand clubbers at Amnesia, is it? Dinner with two other couples in San Antonio?"

To which Lucas simply shrugged and stroked Trevor, the dog.

At the start of the summer season they jumped on Lucas's scooter, put Trevor in a little carry case and drove to Playa D'en Bossa beach to see the sunrise.

"This is my family," Lucas said as he looked from Christopher to the dog and back.

Christopher nodded silently.

They parked the scooter at the quiet end of the beach, away from the big hotels and restaurants. Although strictly speaking they weren't allowed the dog on the beach, they knew they'd be unlikely to be caught this early in the day.

Christopher closed his eyes and meditated in silence for five minutes, preparing himself for a busy summer ahead.

Lucas followed suit, balancing on one leg in a yoga pose he found comfortable that he knew would make Christopher smile beneath semi-closed eyes.

Afterwards, Christopher secured the dog's lead to a stick in the ground next to the clothes they'd stepped out of and then, naked, he held Lucas's hand.

Lucas glanced down at his boyfriend's hairy naked body and felt a jolt of excitement which matched with the gentle warming of the sun on his skin.

Christopher kissed Lucas then, still holding hands they ran into the sea, spraying water, splashing as it reached their knees until finally when it was deep enough, they dived in to swim.

Lucas enjoyed the cool water and freedom of swimming naked—something he'd always wanted to do as a child but had never been allowed by his parents.

The dog barked from afar.

Lucas couldn't believe the letters Christopher had written for him had worked and—as he'd pointed out—the dancing audition Lucas had done afterwards had landed him spots that season in both Amnesia and Pacha, two of Ibiza's biggest clubs. He'd be dancing in front of up to twenty thousand people a night.

Lucas was so lucky to have found this man. The box Maria had bought them had worked. He smiled to himself.

CHRISTOPHER SAW THE smile and swam closer. "What?"

"This, everything, the sun, the water, the empty beach. I'm so happy."

Christopher reflected for a moment. All he had in the world was a little scooter—they'd had to sell the car before the classes had taken off—and an apartment of second hand furniture. If he'd have told the old Christopher what his new job title was, he'd have turned his nose up. Summer content manager for *Ibiza Discovered*—it didn't sound like much compared with President, acquisitions and new business for Europe, which he'd been at the bank. But the important difference now was that he enjoyed writing the reviews, thinking of new ideas to attract other Brits to Ibiza throughout the year.

His tie dyed, dreadlocked friends from the hippy scene would also have repulsed the old Christopher. But now he knew them as real people, he felt blessed to count the knitters, the wood carvers, the fellow spiritualists and the vegans, as friends. They had taught him so much about living a simple life. About taking time to enjoy the moment. Confirming with him that although a new car may feel like a solution to all your problems, actually, it was just a new car, and the solution to your problems was something within yourself. He had put aside his judgements about them since living on Ibiza and enjoyed putting other's feelings before his own through volunteering in the same stray dog shelter which they'd adopted Trevor from.

He never would have believed that the simple pleasures of food, mindfulness and spirituality and finding love with a man who really understood him and loved him back, would make him as happy as they did.

They swam towards one another, kissed and held each other around the waist, their skin touching in the water.

"I love you so much," Christopher said.

"I can't imagine being with anyone else," Lucas replied. "I love you too."

They kissed as the sun rose from the sea, bathing the beach with a gentle golden glow and warmth on their faces.

Acknowledgements

Thanks to everyone at NineStar Press for everything they've done in making this document into a book: giving it an amazing cover – it's just as I imagined it with the two main characters and beautiful Ibiza laid out to tempt you to visit; working with me on a clean insightful edit to make my story sparkle; and everyone involved in the technical side of publishing the book. Thank you all.

Thanks to my beta readers, Victoria Milne, Roe Horvat, and Lillian Francis, who helped me see the wood from the trees, and work out which bits of the story really weren't working and needed to go or be move around. All this, while also being supportive and positive about liking the setting and the characters. The story I submitted was light years better thanks to them both.

Thanks to a publisher whose submission call sparked off the idea for this story. I was having a bit of a blank about what to write next– which is rare for me – and I saw this submission call as we were about to holiday in Ibiza. I thought it would make a perfect setting for the story.

Thanks to my boyfriend, Tim, who put up with me writing quite a lot of this while we were on holiday in Ibiza. While he made dinner, lit the BBQ, prepared salads, I sat by the pool with Monica my trusty Alphasmart Neo and wrote. For his support for this book and all my writing, thank you.

Finally, thanks to you the reader for buying this book. I hope you enjoy a bit of escape into the beautiful island of Ibiza and the emotional romance between these two men.

Love and light,

Liam Livings xx

About the Author

Liam Livings lives where east London ends and becomes Essex. He shares his house with his boyfriend and cat. He enjoys baking, cooking, classic cars and socialising with friends. He has a sweet tooth for food and entertainment: loving to escape from real life with a romantic book; enjoying a good cry at a sad, funny and camp film; and listening to musical cheesy pop from the eighties to now. He tirelessly watches an awful lot of Gilmore Girls in the name of writing 'research'.

Published since 2013 by a variety of British and American presses, his gay romance and gay fiction focuses on friendships, British humour, romance with plenty of sparkle. He's a member of the Romantic Novelists' Association, and the Chartered Institute of Marketing. With a masters in creative writing from Kingston University, he teaches writing workshops with his partner in sarcasm and humour, Virginia Heath as www.realpeoplewritebooks.com and has also ghost written a client's 5 Star reviewed autobiography.

Facebook: www.facebook.com/liam.livings

Twitter: @LiamLivings

Website: www.liamlivings.com

Other books by this author

Adventures in Dating...in Heels

Also Available from NineStar Press

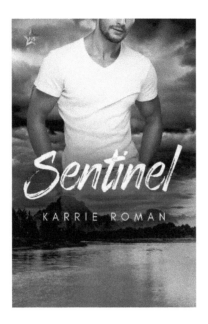

Connect with NineStar Press

Website: NineStarPress.com

Facebook: NineStarPress

Facebook Reader Group: NineStarNiche

Twitter: @ninestarpress

Tumblr: NineStarPress